The World is Dead

By

Mark Harris

Published by

MELROSE BOOKS

An Imprint of Melrose Press Limited
St Thomas Place, Ely
Cambridgeshire
CB7 4GG, UK
www.melrosebooks.co.uk

FIRST EDITION

Cover by Melrose Books

ISBN 978-1-910792-44-5
epub 978-1-910792-45-2
mobi 978-1-910792-46-9

Printed and bound in Great Britain by:
CPI Group (UK) Ltd, Croydon, CR0 4YY

FSC
www.fsc.org
MIX
Paper from
responsible sources
FSC® C013604

To my wife, Tina, my daughter, Tatania
and my grandaughter, Zoe

Prologue

The man boarded the plane, went to his seat, put on his belt and then fell asleep. A female cabin-crew member woke him and told him that the plane had landed in Paris. It was time to get off now. He nodded, undid his belt and walked slowly to the exit.

"Are you alright, sir?" she asked; he was very grey, and there was sweat on his forehead.

Again, he just nodded.

Once off the plane, he caught the train to Calais then got on to the ferry to Dover. He spent most of the voyage either in the toilet being violently sick or fast asleep. The burning in his head was getting worse; sweat was pouring out of him like a running tap. At last, the ferry pulled into port; he wanted to get off as soon as he could.

The air was cool, but he was still sweating. People were starting to look at him – he was swaying about like a man who had too much to drink. As he was walking down the gangway he started to throw up over the side; people tutted and shook their heads.

At customs, he was asked again if he was okay. He told them he was fine: it was just a bad cold, and he needed to get home. Because he looked so ill, the customs personnel just let him go; they didn't want to touch him.

Finally, he was out, and he walked to a park, spied a bench and sat down. *Just five minutes*, he told himself. Then he'd get home and shut his eyes.

And that's when he died.

The park keeper came along a short while later and saw the man on the bench.

"Frickin' hell, another piss head," he said. He walked over to the man. *God* the keeper thought, *he looks dead*, so he shook him. Nothing, he shook him again. "Hey, Buddy, time to go home."

The man's eyes opened; they had a pale look to them, like someone with cataracts. He groaned and started to get up. As he did, he reached out and got hold of the park keeper's jacket. He pulled the man towards him, biting his arm in the process.

"You bastard!" the keeper said as he pushed the man away and ran for the gates.

Chapter One

Where do I start with this tale? I suppose with who I am.

My name is Nick Hutchinson, 'Hutch' to my friends and anyone who knows me. I live in a quiet suburb of Leicester called Glenfield. It has a large superstore, three pubs, some small corner shops, a couple of chippies, three Chinese take-aways, half a dozen hairdressers and two primary schools. It was once a small village, but it's now much bigger. Not quite a town yet, but people still call it a village. At one time it boasted the longest railway tunnel in England – that was in the heyday of steam – but it was closed off now.

I worked as a school caretaker, just doing my job, keeping the school tidy and running. Before that, I was in the armed forces for twenty-five years; toured the world and fought in many conflicts. I reached the rank of Sergeant Major. Once I left the forces, I just wanted the quiet life. So, for the last three years, I worked at the school.

There was an outbreak of an unknown virus in West Africa. It was all over the news; people were dying in their thousands. It seemed to be contained to that area, and the situation was stabilising. For health and safety reasons, news crews were not allowed to travel there to report on the problem. The government was saying that there was no chance of it getting to Britain. The situation was under control.

But it did.

* * *

"Nick," shouted my wife, Rachael, from the living room, "come and see this ... what's on the news."

I came in from the garden, taking my dirty boots off at the door, and walked through the kitchen to the living room. She was standing in front of the television with her hands over her mouth.

"What's up, babes?" I said.

The news had just finished, so I rewound it (thank god for Sky+) to the beginning.

"And today: an unusual disturbance in the port town of Dover, where a man attacked a group of tourists. The attacker bit several of the group, and even tore out the throat of one woman. Police managed to drag the man away and place him in custody. The man, who cannot be named at this moment, is said to have just returned from West Africa, and may have been at the site of the African outbreak. We will provide more information when it is available."

There was a short clip from someone's mobile: it showed the crazed man groaning and snapping at the tourists. He lunged for one of them as the footage cut off, and the program reverted to the newscaster. Looking slightly shocked, the presenter put his hand to his ear, nodded and carried on with the rest of the news.

I stopped the recording and gaped at the screen, which was now playing an advert for breakfast cereal.

"Bloody hell, it's something from a horror film," I said in a whisper.

Rachael just nodded. "What do you think sent him like that?" she asked.

Shaking my head: "No idea, maybe sick with some sort of virus."

That night it was all over the news. The man, whose name was John Pickering, had worked near the virus site in Africa, somehow contracting the disease. They think he was scratched by one of the contaminated when he entered the area. He is still in hospital, in a secure unit, along with the people he attacked. Before attacking the tourists, he went after a park keeper who found him, asleep, on a bench. Police are asking people who may have been in contact with Pickering to come forward so they can be checked for the virus. The airline that flew him to France, along with the ferry company that transported him to Dover, are attempting to contact all passengers.

There is a nationwide panic underway, but the government is still reassuring the country there is nothing to worry about.

What we didn't know at the time was that some infected were brought to the Leicester Royal Infirmary (LRI). It started to spread through the hospital as the affected attacked the staff. The army was brought in to cordon off the area, but they suffered their own bites and scratches as the infected seemed to multiply.

What we know now is *now*. At the time, we didn't realise that people were dying from their wounds and then waking up from the dead. That's when they tried to eat people.

Yes: *eat*.

We first found out about the dead when someone from inside the hospital put a video on Facebook. The government eventually started to panic as the infected escaped the LRI. They brought in more forces and started to shoot the dead, but they just kept coming. The secondary forces, too, started to get over run. That's when they began to use flame throwers.

Even burnt, the affected didn't really die. Some stayed down, but most just kept on moving. Leicester City Centre was overrun within three days, and that's when we found out it had also spread to London and two other major cities.

Chapter Two

Over the next two weeks, Rachael and I started to stock up on tinned food and supplies. We filled our cupboards and spare rooms with the stuff. I even bought gas heaters and lamps with plenty of spare bottles. In my shed, I stored diesel for the car, just in case we needed to make a run for it. I also made some makeshift weapons: axes, swords and the like.

In the back garden, I filled large containers with water and bought sterilising tablets to keep it drinkable. I re-enforced all the doors and put strong bolts on them. The windows were double glazed, so I didn't worry about them, but we put up black-out curtains. A few of our neighbours left to go to safer areas, but I thought it best, for the time being, to stay put and fortify our house. It was in the middle of the street, and the rear gardens were all fenced, so I didn't worry about the backs.

Every day the news got worse; the army were only just keeping the dead from escaping central Leicester. They had built barriers on every road and street to keep them confined. They were still using flame throwers to put them down.

There was also a curfew, people were not allowed out unless they had a permit – otherwise they would be arrested. The phones were still working, so if you needed to go out, you would have to contact a call centre and get a number. You could then leave your home for an allotted two hours. The shops were starting to run dry from everyone trying to stock up. I think we had enough food and supplies to last six months.

4

My daughter, Jess, moved in with us, along with her daughter, Neave. She lived too close to the hospital for comfort, so I brought her in. Her partner, Jason, was stubborn and stayed where he was. Jess pleaded with him to come, but he wanted to stay there. He thought the army would never let the dead get out, or they would wipe them out altogether. I did ask him if he had watched the news.

His reply was: "No way, that's crap." So we left him.

On the third week, all the electric suddenly went. We had no television to keep us updated, so I sat in the car listening to the radio. They had broken out of the cordon, killing the soldiers, and were now moving away from the city centre. I tried the phones, which were still working, and rang the call centre to see what was going on. All I got was the busy tone, so I hung up the phone and called Jason, Jess's partner. There was no answer; it was my last chance to bring him to us, so I tried a few more times, then told Jess to try. I feared he was already dead. Jess kept calling for three days but still no joy.

I told her my fears, and what she did next surprised me: she shrugged her shoulders and said, "I already knew; he had his chance." I gave her a big, daddy hug, and then she started to cry.

Neave, our granddaughter, came over to us and hugging our legs said, "Daddy is ok."

For a three-year old she was very mature. I bent down, picked her up, and gave her a granddad hug. God, I loved these girls. It was up to me to look after them and keep them safe.

My first sighting of – I didn't really know what to call them at the time – the dead ... roamers, was two days later. I had seen one walking down the street. It was a man; hard to tell his age from where I was. I could tell he must have been killed by a pack: his guts were hanging from his stomach. He walked slowly, as though he was drunk. Across the road, I saw a curtain twitch, so I wasn't the only one looking at him.

Four doors down from the curtain twitcher was Mr Holton. He was a very pompous man who lived on the street since it was built in the sixties. He thought he owned it, the way he'd complain about every little thing from noise to road works. I remember one workman telling him to 'fuck off', and 'the job will be finished when it's finished'.

Holton came out of his house with a walking stick. He was walking up to the dead man, and I opened the window to get a better view.

"You have no right to come down here!" he shouted.

The roamer seemed to pick up its pace.

"This is a respectable area, and we don't want the like ..."

The affected went for Holton, stopping him in mid-sentence. They both fell on the floor. Mr Holton started to scream as the man bit into his face, pulling his nose away. Holton's wife came running out and tried to wrestle the dead man off him.

I grabbed my axe and ran out of the house, across the road, towards them. The man was now trying to bite the wife, but she was holding him off and screaming. The man was growling.

When I reached them, I brought the axe down on the creature's head. The blade went straight through his skull, and he fell to the floor. Mrs Holton went over to her husband, who was rolling around holding his nose. I went over to him to see how bad the damage was. I gently pulled his hands away to look: there was no nose left, just a gaping hole full of blood and flesh.

Mrs Holton was starting to get hysterical. I was trying to calm her down, as some of the neighbours came out. The curtain twitcher came over to help Mrs Holton; her husband went to Mr Holton.

"That was stupid of him ..." said the man. I wish I could remember his name at the time, I later found out it was Paul.

"But brave of you to kill it like you did."

I felt a bit stupid myself, now, as I could have been bitten.

"Why does he have to think he runs this street?"

I felt someone touch my arm it was Rachael. "You alright?" she asked.

"Yes, just feeling a bit shaky."

The lady was taking Mrs Holton to her home when her husband, Paul, let out a loud gasp. We turned to him. "He's dead," he said, looking at us.

Mrs Holton heard this and let out a wail of despair. I looked at Paul, and him at me. We both knew what was about to happen. Mrs Holton ran back to her husband, dropping to her knees and bending over him.

Paul and I shouted, "No!" which seemed to shock her. She edged back and looked at us, and then her husband. Shaking her head, she bent down to him again.

I grabbed her arm and said, "He's one of *them* now! When he comes back, he'll kill you!"

She slapped me around the face.

Rachael went to say something, but I shook my head at her, "She's just lost her husband."

She nodded and backed away.

"Rachael, go and get me the duct tape from the house." Once she had gone, I told the crowd, "The Johnsons left to go north. We'll tie him up and put him in their back garden. I'll wait till he turns and do the job."

Everyone patted me on the back, saying what a great bloke I was. Rachael came back, and I asked two of the men to tie Holton. I also told them that if he moved, just to back off, and I'd hit him with the axe. They agreed, and the job was done.

We dragged him into the Johnsons' garden and left him on the grass. Once back outside, I told the people to make sure they were safe and to try to get some weapons. Everyone thanked me, once again, and went back to their houses.

Me? I went into the Johnsons' garden, locked the back gate, and then made an opening in the fence to my yard.

Then I waited.

It was two and a half hours later when I saw his fingers moving, and his eyes opened. They were pale, his face was grey in colour, and he started to groan and hiss. I walked over to him; I had brought a metal stake with me. Standing over him, I placed the stake over his heart and pushed – wow, it was hard. The bones crunched with the force, and then, as it went through the chest cavity, it felt easier; blood leaked out from the hole. He gave a groan, but he was still moving,

What the ... I said to myself. *That should have killed him?*

Then I remembered how I killed the one in the street, so I plunged the stake through his head. Again, the bone was hard to get through; eventually, I felt the brain squish, and he stopped moving.

The brain has to be destroyed to stop these beasts; why weren't we told this on the news? Why didn't the government know this? If they had put a bullet through the heads of the first lot, this may have never happened.

God, I was angry. "Stupid Bastards!" I shouted.

Chapter Three

After that, the dead came down our street nearly every day, but there were only one or two at a time. We'd watch from the top window, just letting them go on their way. When it was quiet, the neighbours and I would meet in the Johnson house to see how everyone was holding up. We also started to work out some emergency plans. The one common question that we kept asking ourselves was: *shall we kill the ones that come down our street; they could hurt someone and make more of those things?*

We agreed that if there were only one or two, then yes, we should. Though I insisted that we go out in force to make it easier; it also lessened the possibility of someone getting hurt. We arranged that if the dead were seen, you should open an upstairs window. When you saw two more open windows, it was time to go out and deal with the beasts.

We made a fire in the back of the Johnsons to burn the bodies; the last things we needed were disease and rats. Paul and I walked the streets in our area to see what was going on. Most of the people had left, but we did find some dead bodies. We even started to build a barricade at both ends of the street. It did its job; the dead couldn't get through. Out of the forty or so houses on the street, eleven were occupied. We arranged guard duty on the barricades.

We all felt safe and comfortable in our little fort. We shared our supplies, so no one went hungry. Every couple of days a few of us would go around looking for food and provisions in the empty houses and shops. We never saw any other people – the whole place seemed like a ghost town. All the shops in the area had been gutted; there must have been riots in the end. When we met the dead, we swiftly dispatched them, but if there was a large group, we'd work our way around them or even backtrack. There seemed to be more and more of them every day.

Each time we went out, we would have to go further away to find anything useful. One day we had to take a car. We took a small hatchback to save fuel. My car was the only diesel, so we siphoned off all the petrol we could find and stored it in jerrycans. On our trips, we collected more containers so we could store more fuel. You can never have too much.

We had to fight for our lives on one such trip to the hospital in Glenfield, losing one of our group to the dead.

We drove to the hospital after we started to run low on some medical supplies. The drive over was quiet. We cut through the estate to the main dual carriageway, driving on it in the wrong lane.

"Always wanted to do that," I laughed as we got to the traffic island.

We drove slowly into the grounds and noticed a few of the dead walking around the car park. I pulled the car up to the main doors, which were closed, and killed the engine. In the front seat, next to me, was my new best friend, Paul, and in the back were Arron, Keith and Joanne.

"Arron, you stay here in the car, and get it going the second you see us. We may need to leave pretty fast," I said. Arron climbed back in and nodded; he looked very scared. "If you see trouble, sound the horn, and we'll come straight back. If you have to move, meet us at the south entrance. Keep circling if you have to; we'll wait inside till you pull up, OK?"

He replied with an OK.

We turned to the building; each took a deep breath, then we pulled the doors open and went inside, closing them behind us.

All the lights were out, and it was very dark. We waited a couple of minutes just to see if anything was near us. I could hear the groans of the dead somewhere in the building, but couldn't place them. Looking up at the signs, I found which way to go to get to the pharmacy. I put my fingers to my lips as if to say 'no noise', and off we went.

It wasn't far, but it took a long time getting there – we checked every room as we went. We didn't want the dead coming from behind. After every check, we'd close the door and draw a cross on it. That way we knew it was clear.

In one room, we found a dead one in a wheelchair; it hissed at us as we entered. It was an old lady – she must have been about 80. Joanne put her diver's knife through its head and then said, "There's no bite marks; she's clean."

"How come she's one of them if she wasn't bitten?" Keith asked in reply.

We checked her neck, arms and legs. Joanne pulled the woman's dress up, and there were no bites anywhere. It was strange. We left her there and closed the door.

Around the next corner there were two of them just standing there, looking our way. I put up three fingers and did a countdown. On the last finger, we ran round the corner and took them out – Paul with the axe and me with a sword. Joanne ran ahead to the pharmacy, which was in the next door.

"*Joanne*," I hissed as she ran straight into a pack of about nine dead.

She screamed in fright as one lunged for her. Both Paul and Keith ran forwards, with me following. Joanne had killed the one that grabbed her, but two more were on her. Paul brought the axe down on one, and Keith got the other with his iron stake. I cut two more down with a massive swing of the sword, then reversed just in time to get one that was nearing from behind. Joanne screamed again as one got her around the neck – Keith put the stake through its head. Paul swung his axe and took the head off another. I took out the last by kicking it in the leg, which made it fall over, and plunging the sword down through its skull.

We all looked around at each other taking deep breaths. "God that was close," said Keith.

"Fucking hell, Jo, you know the rules," whispered Paul.

"Sorry, guys," she said, "I saw the pharmacy and thought it was safe ... sorry ..."

"It's ok, just don't do it again," I said smiling at her. "Good work out though."

"Right, let's get the stuff: remember, we need antibiotics, painkillers, ointment, antiseptics and bandages. So fill up your backpacks and any other bags you find. Jo, you're on lookout; give me your pack and I'll fill it."

She said 'right' and waited at the door.

We started by clearing the room to make sure it was safe. We found the pharmacist. She was standing at the back of the room holding a prescription. She came at us, and Keith put his stake through her eye. It exploded and covered him in blood and juice. "Shit, that stinks!" he said, while wiping his face on the sleeve of his coat. We gave a little titter and got on with our work.

Fifteen minutes later, our packs were full and heavy, and we had two carrier bags each. We started to make our way back to the entrance. Knowing the rooms were clear, we just had to check around corners, so it was quicker. Until we got to the lobby.

There must have been forty of the beasts standing there, looking out of the doors. Some at the front were trying to scratch their way through the glass, but it held. From where we were, I could see Arron in the car, but he was looking around at the car park and not at the entrance. If he turned, he would see the dead at the door and know we were in trouble. Then he would move to the south entrance. We decided to head to the south entrance regardless, hoping he would soon see the dead and move on to meet us.

None of us had ever gone to the south entrance before, so we started to work our way through the maze of the hospital. Knowing the way we just came was clear, we used it as a starting point and quickly got back to the pharmacy. I told everyone to store their carrier bags in a room. If we came back at a later date we could retrieve them; right now, we needed our hands free to carry our weapons.

Again, we had to clear rooms as we went, but only rooms with doors open. Once cleared, we closed them and marked them as before. We only saw one or two dead at a time and easily dispatched them. It took us over an hour to get to the south entrance, with a lot of doubling back each time we came to a dead end.

In the lobby of the south entrance were five dead. Luckily, all of them were at the door, trying to get out. We each picked one and went forward. I indicated that I'd take the two on the right – off we went.

Slowly moving towards them, I decided to take the outer one first, hoping to knock the second down with the same blow. Then I'd put my sword through its head. Joanne was the first to strike, plunging her diver's knife into the temple of the one on the left. Keith went in with his stake; Paul and I attacked at the same time.

As I swung the sword to cut the head off my target, it turned and started to move towards me. My aim was out, and I took its arm off at the shoulder. The second was now moving towards Paul, who had problems with the axe. He had hit his beast so hard that he cleaved the head in two – the axe was jammed, stuck in its neck and shoulders.

I backed away and took another swing at mine. The top of its head went flying, and the thing dropped to the floor. The second one was now on Paul, who had let go of his axe. Both Joanne and Keith were on it, stabbing wildly. Finally, Joanne got it in the head, pushing her knife through the back of its skull.

"Shit shit shit ..." said Paul, holding his hand to his chest.

With all the blood that covered him and us, it was hard to see what the problem was till he held out his hand. There was a chunk missing from between his thumb and forefinger.

"Sorry Paul, but I'm going to chop off the hand."

His eyes widened, and he shook his head.

"It might be the only way to save you. Keith, hold him down."

"Nick, you can't!" said Joanne.

"We have to try before the infection gets a grip."

Paul kneeled down on the floor, holding his arm to the ground – Keith held it steady. Joanne start to cry but also emptied her pack for bandages and antiseptic cream. I retrieved Paul's axe and took aim. I swung it down and took his hand clean off; he wailed and fainted. Joanne quickly put pressure on the stump and started to wrap it in bandages.

I heard the noise of the dead from somewhere down the corridor, they must have heard Paul's agonised howl. Then, outside, I saw Arron pull up in the car. He was looking hard to find us. I told Keith and Joanne to open the doors before he pulled away. I managed to get Paul over my shoulders in a fireman's lift and carried him out to the car. Joanne helped me get Paul into the back seat; Keith tried to hold him up.

Just as Joanne was about to get in, Arron shouted to look behind us. There was a pack of the dead coming out of the entrance. I shouted for Joanne to get in quick, but Paul's unconscious body was in the way. Keith tried harder to pull him upright, but it was too late.

One of the dead grabbed Joanne by the hair, and pulling her back, bit into the side of her face, pulling her cheek flesh away. She gave an agonising yowl while another took a bite out of her neck. She was soon covered in them.

I went to get out of the car, but Keith screamed, "No Nick, she's dead!"

And she was.

Arron put the car in gear, and we flew away from the scene at speed. The drive back was in silence.

Chapter Four

"There was nothing we could do," I told Terry, Joanne's partner. "We got swarmed by them. We had all got to the car, but Joanne was just unlucky. I tried to help, but we all would have died, and she took a bite before we could even get back out," I explained.

"He's been bit," he said, pointing to the Johnson house.

We put Paul in there and tied him to a bed to be safe. If he turned then the deed would be done. As for now he was asleep.

"We'll see what happens, when it happens, with Paul. Rose is watching over him now and will tell us when he wakes up or dies." There was a moment of silence.

"We've lost a valuable member of the team, she was gutsy and brave ..."

We were quiet again for a while, thinking of Joanne. Terry and she moved into the street three years ago. She was a teacher; he, an office manager at some law firm. They never wanted children, so that was why they never married. She was thirty-five and he was thirty-eight.

"Tomorrow, I'll take someone over to the hospital and try to find her, if she's turned, I ..." I paused, trying to think of the right words. "I'll just bring her back, and we'll bury her in the house at the end. It's got a big garden."

David Holms, a large, quiet man, said he would come, as he felt useless. I nodded, and we arranged to go in the morning.

David and I went the next day. I told people that we'd only get out of the car if we saw Joanne. We drove to the attack site: there was a lot of blood on the ground where Joanne went down but no sign of her. I saw a group of the dead, so I took my binoculars and tried to look for her. I could tell she wasn't with them. We drove around the whole site, and there was no sight of her, so we went home.

As we pulled off the dual carriageway, David stopped the car. I looked at him.

"Look," he said, pointing out the back window. We waited a few seconds then a car went by, it looked full of people.

"When did you see them?"

"They came off the roundabout, just before we turned in. I still use the mirror," he smiled.

"Wonder who they are?" I asked.

He just shrugged his shoulders and said that he hoped they were friendly. It was a red car, and it looked like a Volvo with its square shape.

When we arrived back, we told them about the sighting. We also told them that we couldn't find Joanne.

"Well, I'm going to find her," asserted Terry.

"Come off it," said Rachael, "she's dead or one of them."

"I need to do this." With that, he went to his home, packed his backpack, took an iron stake and a knife, and off he went. No one stopped him; what was the point?

That left ten households. There was us: Rachael, Jess, Neave and me. There were Paul and Rose, and Mrs Holton – she never came out, Rachael and Rose did check on her, but she just wailed behind closed doors. Keith and his wife, Mary, lived up the road. Mary is a great cook; she set up a gas barbeque and prepared all the food for the group. Arron and his partner, Julie, are good kids, and help where they can. Then there's Steve and Kelly, a great couple who also muck in with the chores. David Holm and Marie: David was in the building business, and Marie worked for him. Tony and Jayne were the last of the young couples. Tony was pretty good at building things; he kept the barricades in good condition with the help of David. Finally, we have the oldies of the group: Tom and Flo, Ralph and Mable, and Josie, who was a widow. They keep our spirits up with their stories and good humour. They also helped Mary a lot and sorted the supplies, keeping them in check, telling us what we needed and when.

Time seemed to have lost all meaning now; all we knew was morning, midday and night. Days just blended into nothing. If you asked me the day, I couldn't have told you. The weather was starting to get cooler, so I knew that autumn was on its way. It felt a lifetime since the first outbreak, but it was only two and half months ago. Rachael kept a calendar and marked off the days. When I asked her why, she told me that she needed some of the old life to cling to, or she'd go mad.

We made one of the empty houses into a communal eating area where we would go for breakfast, lunch and dinner. We all went back to our homes for sleep and alone time, and it worked quite well. Tony and David connected the gas to the house's mains, so Rose had the use of a cooker. We turned one of the rooms into a meeting area so we could sit and talk in the warmth; winter was coming. We even thought about a generator for electric, so we could have light, but decided that our gas lamps would have to suffice – we would have to use fuel to power a generator. There was nothing to listen to now, as even the radio stations were dead. Every day I'd sit in my car and try to find something, but there was nothing – just static.

We knew Britain had gone to the dead, but we didn't know about the rest of the world. Had they contained it in Africa? As we were an island, could they contain it here? We had no way of knowing, so we just tried to survive.

Paul was starting to recover from his bite and the amputation of his hand. Tony fixed him with a metal stump-cover that brandished a deadly looking hook. Even though he seemed in good nature, he did act differently after the incident. Sometimes, there was a coldness to him, particularly when we went out to find supplies. He would go after the dead with a vengeance – there was hate on his face when he'd kill one, and he'd smile when he finished.

We were also starting to worry about Mrs Holton; none of us had seen her since that first day. Even though the women would try and get her out, they said she was still moaning, hissing and wailing.

It was Keith who wanted to knock the door down, see how she was and get her some help.

I was sitting in my back garden, just chilling in the last of the year's warm sun, when I heard the scream. I ran through the house to the front, grabbing my sword on the way. Once outside, I looked left and right to see where the noise came from. Tony and David were rushing to Mrs Holton's with their weapons. Mable came staggering around the corner of the house, holding her neck and weeping. Next came Keith, holding his shoulder. Even from where I was, I could see blood running down his jumper.

"She's one," he called out as he came up to me.

I saw Ralph taking his wife into his arms just as she collapsed. She was covered in blood, and it soon covered him. Her skin had gone grey, and she had fallen quiet. I feared the worst for her.

Keith was telling me what had happened, when Mrs Holton came around the corner of the house. She was a very thin lady to start with, but now she was skeletal – her face was so drawn that you could see her skull through the taut skin. The thing that was Mrs Holton lumbered over towards the group that gathered around Mable's body. I shouted a warning, but they were focussed on Mable and Ralph.

I shouted once again and started running, but it was too late for Arron. He turned at the last second, and Holton bit into his neck, pulling the skin away and severing the jugular. Blood squirted a good four metres as he pushed her away, eventually falling to the ground from the loss. I ran over to her and pushed my sword through her temple; she dropped immediately.

Ralph yelled, the sound transforming into a gurgle. When we got to him, Mable had turned and ripped his throat out. There was blood everywhere, over everyone and everything. Again, I did the deed with the sword.

Ralph had collapsed over Mable, so I put the sword through his head too; I didn't want him to turn. I then walked over to Arron and raised the sword.

Julie screamed, "No!" I stopped and looked at her.

"He's still alive; he might survive!" she pleaded.

"He'll be dead soon, and when he is he will turn – plus, he's in pain. It's the best thing to do ..."

She ran over to him, kissing him and telling him things were alright. He moaned something to her, then raised his head and bit her. The bite from Mrs Holton had killed him outright, and we didn't see it happen. He had already turned. Keith and I ended them both.

Keith then turned to me: "Take me to the Johnson house, tie me up. I want you to do it, mate."

"Why me?" I asked.

"I trust you not to let me turn. I don't want to be one of them for even a second."

"Alright, I'll do it."

So I walked with him over to the Johnsons', after telling

the others to take the dead down to the bottom house and bury them.

Keith and I went into the garden and sat on patio chairs, chatting.

"I'm not tying you up; once you've gone, then I'll do the job. I'll make it quick."

"Cheers Buddy," he nodded. "Why did they turn so quick? Holton took a few hours after he was dead."

"I did wonder that myself," I replied. "Maybe the adrenalin in the system sped it up?"

"Maybe that's why the city was overrun so quick. If the dead started attacking, it would scare the shit out of you, so your adrenalin would be pumping like mad," Keith surmised.

"But Holton was quite angry when that roamer got him, so why not him?" I wondered.

"Because he's all bluster: he put on pretence, hence no adrenalin."

"How are you feeling?" I asked.

"Okay, why?"

"I'm going to get some beer, it's too nice to sit here and not drink beer," I said. "I'll be back in a minute."

"Lock the gate and doors after you, just in case."

"I won't be long."

"Just do it," he said in a stern tone.

I said OK and went for the beers.

I also fetched some bandages, antiseptic and painkillers to help him. On returning, I went through the house, stopping when I got to the French window. I saw him slumped in his chair. *Shit*, I thought: my sword was out there next to my chair. I looked around the kitchen for something sharp to use, but we'd already taken the knives. I looked around the house and found a screwdriver in one of the bedrooms.

21

Going back to the window, I saw he was still in the chair. I slowly opened the door and quietly walked over to him, his back towards me. I could hear a low moan coming from him. I put my hand on his shoulder, ready to push the screwdriver through his temple.

He jumped up, almost knocking me over. I was just about to try and stab him through the eye when he said: "What the fuck, Nick? I'm not dead yet!"

"You stupid bastard," I said. "I nearly shat myself. I thought you were dead!"

"I must have nodded off; I'm feeling shattered," he said, "and where's the beer?"

"Inside, I'll fetch them." I went back inside to get the beer and first aid kit.

After sorting his wound out, we sat and chatted for a few hours, the sun was starting to set, so we moved inside as the air was getting colder.

"I feel so sleepy," said Keith, putting his feet on the settee.

"It's been a long day," I replied.

His eyes closed, and he started to snore. I reached for the screwdriver and waited for the snoring and breathing to stop. I would wait for one minute after to make sure he was dead. I didn't worry about him turning straight away, as he was relaxed.

Twice I nearly nodded off, the smell of the gas lamps and the soft glow they gave off was too relaxing. I got up and walked around, looking out of windows. I checked the front and back doors, they were locked. Then I went to the living room, and Keith was breathing quite heavy. I went to the window and looked out: the lights were on in the community house. I suddenly realised how hungry I was. So I went back to the chair to wait. Ten minutes later, there was a knock on the front door. Checking Keith, I went to the window and saw Jess carrying something.

"Hi, Dad, brought some food for you both," she handed it through the window. "How is he?"

"Asleep, he's been like that for the last hour," as I turned to him his breathing stopped. "You go, babes, I don't want you here when I have to do it."

"Alright, Dad, love you, and be careful."

"Love you, too."

She ran back to the community house. I shut the window and went over to him. I pulled the screwdriver out and leaned in a little to see if he had stopped breathing. He had. I pushed the screwdriver in, only a little blood came out. I left him there till the morning, when I would bury him.

Chapter Five

We had a funeral for the dead the next day. It was a very sad affair; we had lost a big chunk of the group, and we felt it. Kelly and Jayne were comforting Mary, who was in total shock. Tom led the service; he was a kind and worldly man – always knew what to say and when to say it. Afterwards, we all went to our homes to be with our loved ones. Josie, the widow, went with Mary and stayed with her. Over the next few days, Flo took over the cooking. Mary helped when she could, but she didn't have the heart to do it anymore.

I was playing with Neave in her bedroom; I didn't get a lot of time with her these days. She had me sitting on the smallest chair, having tea with all her toys. She used to love watching the Disney channel; her favourite programs were *Doc McStuffins* and *Sheriff Callie*. So, over the years we had bought her the stuffed toys of the characters.

It was great to be laughing again; I seemed to have not truly smiled or laughed in months. Neave was my world, as was her mother, and even *her* mother. I would kill for them or die trying. Neave's laugh was so innocent, and in these times it was gold.

The sound of a car horn made me look towards the window. Being so low, all I saw was sky.

"Granddad, what's that noise?" she asked, also looking at the window. She suddenly went all quiet – she knew of the troubles in the world now.

"Not sure, Princess, Granddad's going out to see. You stay here, and see if Stuffy the dragon will drink his tea." With that, I left her, shutting the bedroom door behind me.

At the bottom of the stairs, I picked up my army webbing that carried my knives, my first-aid kit and my sword.

Paul was coming out of his house at the same time, as were others. Tony was on the east barricade: he shouted that there was a red Volvo outside and they wanted to come in. David was on the west side. He called to see if we needed help. I shouted back for him to stay where he was.

A man climbed out of the car. He was filthy and looked very worn down. I could make out two more people in the car; it looked like a woman and another man.

There was a crowd gathering now, all looking at the car and people inside. The man came to the barricade and asked who the leader was. Everyone looked at me.

I must have had a strange look on my face, as Jayne said, "Well, you are, you just sort of took over and did things. We're happy to follow."

Wow, this was news to me. I walked closer and asked what he wanted.

"We need you to let us in and feed us," there was a tone I didn't like. "And to house us, we've been on the road for weeks; half our group are dead."

"Were you in this area about four weeks ago?" I asked

"Yes, was that your car in the hospital? We lost you just as we came off the island. We tried every road off there, but couldn't find you. But now we have, bless god."

I thought for a moment. "Tell the others to get out of the car," I ordered.

"Why?" his eyes narrowed and he stole a glance back at the car.

"Because I said so, and I want their hands up, no weapons," again, it was not a request.

He flicked his head – from nowhere, about ten people came rushing towards us. The man in the car got out and joined the attack. I pulled a knife from my belt and threw it at the man that had done the talking. I got him in the throat; he fell to the floor trying to hold the blood in.

I shouted to my people to get to the cars and make for the other end. That's when David came running up and said we had trouble back there too. *Shit, shit, shit!* Tony, Paul, David and I started fighting off the attackers, killing at least seven of them. The last few backed away as we held our ground. I could hear the cars starting up and also shouts of the attackers from the other end.

I turned around to see another ten or so people running towards us carrying weapons: pointed sticks and clubs. We ran towards them shouting and screaming, some of them stopped, but the others still came at us. I swung my sword and sliced into a man's chest – he fell. Paul and the others also took down one each.

I called my comrades to the cars; the three remaining attackers, plus the two from the Volvo, were closing in. We jumped into the nearest vehicles and attempted to make our escape.

Our cars were getting hit with clubs; people even tried to jump on to them. Our drivers floored it, and we were gone, knocking the stragglers over as we went. The first car ploughed through the barricade. As I looked back, I saw some of the dead rising and attacking the living. I smiled a little and thought: *justice*.

After a few minutes I told Jayne, who was driving, to overtake the lead car and stop. I climbed out and signalled for the others to get out of their cars too. Everyone was talking and making a lot of noise. I asked for quiet and also asked if everyone was alright. I made sure everyone was there.

I was surprised how everyone acted so quickly. We had four cars altogether, and no one was hurt. I looked back down the street the way we came – no one was following.

"Frigging hell, Nick, that was a fantastic knife throw!" said Steve. "Where'd you learn to do that?" he asked.

"I was in the army in my younger days," I replied, not wanting to say any more.

Paul weighed in: "That was too close; we could have all been killed. They didn't even try to talk."

I nodded. "We need guns," I said, just staring down the street.

I wished we could go back, but there must have been at least twenty of the monsters now. Would they walk off, or just hang around like we'd seen before?

"This isn't America, buddy," said Paul, "there's nowhere to get them from."

"I know where to get some," I said, "but it's going to be dangerous."

Chapter Six

It was getting quite heated, with me just standing in the middle being told that I was a fool. The group asked how the hell was I going to get guns? They also insisted that we couldn't start killing the living. Jess walked into the middle with Neave in her arms, and everyone seemed to go quiet. She turned around in the circle, a look of disgust in her eyes.

"I trust my dad with our lives," she said, hugging Neave to her, "and he's done a lot for this group: going out most days looking for food, defending us from those monsters. OK, we lost a few in the time we've been together, but that's not his fault." She paused. "I will go where my dad goes, because he knows things others don't, and I know he'll never let me down." She stood there with tears in her eyes. Rachael walked into the group and held my hand, she also had tears rolling down her cheeks.

"Thanks, babes," I said to Jess, as I went over and kissed her forehead, then Neave's. I pushed my way out of the group and headed with my girls for one of the cars.

"Eh, Nick." I turned, it was Paul. "You saved my life; I'm coming with you."

With that, everyone said that they would stick with me, that I knew what was best. There was a lot of apologising.

"Right, buddy," said David, "so where are these bloody guns?"

I turned to them all and said that we needed to find somewhere safe first, then I would tell everyone my thoughts.

As I climbed into the car, an idea hit me for a safe haven. So I drove, with the others following, to the next village – there was a small castle with a moat. I knew that if it was clear it should be easy to defend. The journey was quiet; we saw no dead or any other life.

The castle was situated on the edge of the village, so we didn't need to drive through it. As we pulled into the car park, I saw it was clear. I told Rachael and Jess to stay and got out of the car. I went over to the others and asked Paul, Tony, and Steve to come with me. I told David to wait with the cars.

We first checked the kiosk: locked and empty. There was a bridge over the moat; it was a good fifteen metres wide and very sturdy. I turned to look at the view behind. I could tell we'd see anyone coming way before they got to us.

The gates were locked with a chain and padlock, so I sent Tony to the kiosk to break in to find the key. I warned him not to make too much noise. Using his steel stake, he wedged it in between the door jam and handle: the door flew inwards. After a few moments he came out with a bunch of keys.

When he got back to us, he went to the lock, and on the third try got the right key. We pushed open one side of the double gates and walked in, closing it behind us. It wasn't a very big area, and it had no roof, but at either side of the gate was a small, covered room. They were not very large, but they were dry, and they provided enough room for us all.

We then walked over to the moat and saw that it was about four or five metres deep. No one would get in that way; it went around the whole castle. Just by standing in the middle of the ruins, I could tell there was no one there.

I left Paul and Tony at the gates, while I went back to the cars. I told the drivers to pull in through the gate, turn the cars facing out, and block the entrance with them. I scanned the area and saw one of the dead ambling up the drive to the castle. It was alone, so I left it. I then went back inside and locked the gates once everyone was in.

Weeks ago, we started to put provisions in the cars, just in case of a quick getaway. Each car had food, fuel and sleeping bags, plus first-aid kits and weapons. We each found a space in the guard room, as we called it. It was still light, so it must have been afternoon.

Was that all? It seemed days since I was playing with Neave, but that was only this morning. We'd need heat for when the night came, so Paul, Steve and I went on a wood hunt. We killed the one outside of the ruins, as it could be a nuisance and draw more to us. We were quite lucky: there was a farm nearby. We had to kill two of the dead there. Then we loaded the car up and headed back – I found a deadly hedging tool, so we took that with us.

Just as dusk was falling, we sat around, eating tinned food warmed up from a large fire. Jayne stood guard on the parapet, overlooking the front of the castle. She had a good view all around us. I started to lay out my plan.

"As I said earlier, it's going to be dangerous; I will only take volunteers." I paused and looked at the group. They were quiet, all staring at me.

"So where are they, mate?" said Paul.

"In the city."

The silence was deafening; there was a look of incredulity on their faces.

"The city was cordoned off after the outbreak, and a lot of the people died. So did the soldiers, and they had guns: rifles, pistols, machine guns and body armour." Once again, a pause.

"Like I said: dangerous. Also, there's a T.A. Centre there, and they have an armoury, so that means plenty of ammo."

Steve gave a low whistle.

I carried on: "But it could take days to get there, with all the dead that will be around the nearer we get. We'll take a car with us and move as close as we dare, then walk the rest." Looking around the group, I could see some were interested, others were scared.

"Once we get to the T.A. Centre, we can get an army vehicle and drive it back. On the plus side, once we get into the area, we might find guns before we get there. That will help us if we get in trouble."

I finished off my meal, which had gone cold, but I didn't mind. I did miss the cooked stuff we had back on the street. Maybe we'd get back there one day.

It was starting to get late. I arranged the guard through the night and then went to bed myself.

It felt like a blink when someone shook me awake, whispering my name. I lifted myself up. It was Flo, she had tears on her cheeks. I asked her what the matter was. She asked if she could talk to me. So I checked Rachael and the others and crawled out of my sleeping bag. It was freezing as I was only wearing my boxer shorts; I grabbed my clothes and walked out with Flo.

We sat near the fire. It was only embers now, but it was warm. "How can I help?" I asked.

"Tom's dying," she said. "He's been ill for many years and has to have tablets to help him, but we ran out just after all this started. I know we should have told you, but you have other problems to deal with. We didn't want to burden you with it."

I was angry with her: *my God, what if he died and killed her and the rest of the group, like Mrs Holton?* I didn't voice these thoughts.

"You should have told us. We could have got them from the hospital when we went." I paused; I was a little harsh. I reached for her hand and in a gentler tone asked, "How long do you think he has?"

"Maybe about a week if we don't get him his pills."

"Right, tomorrow I'll go to the chemist and see if they have them. Do you know what they are called?"

She told me their name.

"Off to bed and keep warm, I'll see you in the morning." I gave her a hug.

She smiled, "Oh, a hug from a young man!" She squeezed back, and then she went to Tom.

Paul and I walked down Main Street to the chemist. We only saw three dead and killed them swiftly. We passed a restaurant, which was at the end of the road leading to the castle, and I said we'd have to go in there later and check it for food. He agreed.

On reaching the chemist we found the door unlocked, so we went in – me with my sword at the ready, and Paul with the hedging tool held high. There were two dead in the shop, so we took one each. I brought down the sword and cleaved the head of mine in two. Paul swung the tool and took the head off his monster, then stamped down, crushing the skull. Brains and blood exploded out with a crunching, squishing sound.

Going to the back of the shop, we found the pharmacist on the floor, eaten in two. Her top half was still alive and reaching for us, hissing and groaning. Paul took her out, then we started to look for our shopping list of tablets. I also wanted to top-up the first-aid kits and antibiotics.

Before we left the site, I asked if anyone else needed anything. Josie said she needed warfarin for her heart, and Jayne asked for some contraception pills, as did Kelly and Rachael. I looked at Marie, and David said, "Had the snip, mate," and we laughed.

After twenty minutes, we found all we needed and headed

back to the castle. I started to wonder if the dead could sense us in some way. I knew noise attracted them, but there seemed to be more of them on the way back. Both Paul and I were quiet on the way in and on the return, but they were coming from the side streets. I counted eighteen of them between us and the ruins. They were slow and far apart, so we dispatched them with ease.

By the time we'd dealt with them we were covered in blood and brains. As Paul took out the last one, I turned to survey the way we came. Even more of the things were following, so we ran the rest of the way to the castle. Tony was on guard and saw us coming. He called for the gate to be opened, and we ran through; the massive doors were shut behind us.

"My goodness, look at you both," said Mary, coming to greet us both with a cup of tea.

While we were gone, the group got the fire going again and made a cooking area. They used tin cans as pots to boil the water. I took mine and had a sip. It was good, but I could have done with something a little stronger, even at this time of the morning.

I went over to Tom and gave him his pills; he was starting to look grey. I told him to take it easy for a few days and build his strength back up. I also told him to give us plenty of warning when he started to run low again. We might not be so lucky next time. He gave a sheepish smile, thanked me and said he wouldn't be so silly in the future.

Flo hugged me, even while I was covered in blood and viscera. I squeezed her, and I said to her, "Oh, hugged by a sex symbol!"

"I wish ..." she said. She patted my bum and smiled, we laughed.

You need to laugh in times like these, even if it is dark or strange humour.

Paul and I washed ourselves in the moat and then sat by the fire to warm up. Rachael came over and took the tablets and pills to hand out and store. I told Paul of my thoughts about the dead sensing us. He agreed.

"I thought that yesterday, when that one came walking up the path, how did it know we were here? And when we came out of the chemist there were loads of them; do you think they can smell us?" he said, taking a breath.

"Later, I want to try something when we go to the restaurant," I said.

"And what may that be?"

"I'm going to cover myself in dead juice: kill one of them things and put its guts all over me. Then I'll walk right through them."

"No way, mate, I can't let you do that." He paused, "I'm doing it. You've got a family – plus I'd want you to back me up if it went wrong."

We agreed to the plan but didn't tell anyone till we were ready to go. After lunch, I asked for volunteers to go to the restaurant to search for food and supplies. Paul, I didn't need to ask, as we had already sorted our strategy. David was the first to come forward, then Steve and Kelly. Tony also agreed, but I said I wanted him and Jayne to stay and look after the site. Jess asked if she could come, as she felt useless just sitting around. I wanted to say no, as she was my baby, but she was also a strong woman. She was twenty three, only four-years younger than Kelly.

I said, "Yes, but you stay close to me and do as I say, right?"

She nodded, "Of course, dad, that's a no-brainer." She gave me one of her 'I love you, daddy' smiles.

Outside the castle were four of the monsters. I readied everyone. We opened the gates and killed them very quickly.

"Jess, grab that one," I pointed to the nearest roamer. "Kelly, you help her, take it to the kiosk. Steve, David, you stand guard, we won't be long."

Jess was not squeamish; she and Kelly dragged the dead beast to the kiosk. Paul led the way inside, and I followed. There was a look of puzzlement on several faces, but no one asked any questions.

Once inside, I sent the girls out and shut the door. Then Paul and I chopped the body up, smearing him in the resultant gore. The smell was foul; I nearly gagged at one point. Paul just stood there as if it was a fashion show. Once finished, he turned on the spot and said, "Does my bum look big in this?"

"You twat," I said, laughing, "you look *gore*-geous!" emphasizing the gore. We both laughed – Jess put her face to the glass to see what we were laughing at. Seeing Paul dressed in his gore suit, her face made us laugh even more. When we calmed down, we left the kiosk and told the party our plan. Right on cue, one came round the corner.

"It's now or never," said Paul, and he walked toward the beast.

We hung back but had our weapons ready to go; Paul opted to remain armed as well. What happened next amazed us all: he walked right up to it and looked it in the face – it just ignored him. He even circled it and got right up close; it just pushed him out the way. We waited till it neared us; it started to pick up speed, hissing and groaning, gnashing its teeth. Then it lunged for me, so I put a knife through it's forehead and it dropped.

Paul walked back to us. "It works," he said, smiling.

"Damn right it does! This is gonna help when we go to the city, but ..." I paused, "I want to try it on a hoard of them."

"Right then, I'm up for that," Paul was actually excited. "There were some on Main Street yesterday, so let's go and find out!"

"No, let's check out the restaurant first. I want a bigger group of us, just in case something goes wrong."

Paul agreed with me, "OK, buddy, I see where you're coming from. Let's go," he turned and started to walk away. I had the feeling he was upset about it, but I didn't worry – the safety of the group came first.

We saw three more dead on the way, and Paul just walked up to them. He circled, and then put his hooked hand through their heads, dropping them where they stood, one by one.

Arriving at the restaurant, we could see it had been ransacked. There were dead on the floor. They had not turned; they had been hacked to pieces. We looked around and found a few tins of fruit, but most of everything was gone. I wondered if it was the group that attacked us. Maybe they had been here – it must have been done by quite a few people, the way the bodies were hacked up like this.

We headed back to the castle with our meagre pickings. We met no dead on the return trip, which again seemed to upset Paul. Since his hand was bitten, he had become more reckless and sometimes cold. I resolved to have a word with Rose about him. I didn't want any mistakes that would harm the group.

We all sat around the fire that night and discussed how we would get into the city. I would only take those that wanted to come. But everyone *did* want to be involved in the mission. So I had to make a choice. I instructed the older ones that they had to stay. I told them that there was no offence intended; we might have to do a lot of running and fighting. Their safety wasn't guaranteed. Also, Neave couldn't go, and someone had to look after her, so that was their job.

I needed someone strong to look after the castle as well, so I elected Paul, Rose, Tony and Jayne. The rest would come with me. Paul tried to argue the point, and I told him I needed someone I could trust to make the right decisions. Tony and Jayne had to stay, as they were very versatile at doing things, but they needed Paul's leadership.

Before we went, I wanted to make sure the gore suit worked, so we opted to do some supply runs and try it out. I knew there was a camping place nearby. We'd go there first to get warm bedding and gas stoves to cook by. Then we would try a supermarket to get food. Also, we would do a hospital run for more tablets for Tom and Josie, but we'd try local chemist's first.

Over the next few days, we worked on the plan. I let Steve, Kelly, David and Marie do the camping store run on their own. I needed to trust people to be able to work without me. Before they left, we killed a couple of beasts and put them in the boot of their car. Once they arrived at their destination, they were to chop them up and cover themselves in the gore. On the supermarket trip, I let Rachael and Jess go with Paul, and they did the same.

When Paul left the castle I asked Rose for a chat.

We sat next to the fire, and she made me a cup of coffee. I asked her how she and Paul were.

"Why do you ask?" she said, slightly tilting her head.

I had to think for a second: "He's not the Paul I knew before his hand was bitten. He goes out there, wanting to kill them things, doing the dangerous stuff just for kicks. I'm worried for him."

"Yes, he has changed, but haven't we all?" Rose said softly. "When, in normal life, do the dead start walking, and we have to kill them to survive?" A tear formed in the corner of her left eye, she wiped it away.

"I know, it's hard for us all, but I need to trust Paul not to get us killed. That's why I'm leaving him here: to look after everyone I trust. He'll do that well, but outside I feel he may run into trouble. Trouble that he can't get out of. Then it'll cause us more problems." I dropped my eyes from hers. I felt guilty about what I said. It is hard to hear bad things about a loved one.

"Yes, I know. He tells me he just wants to get out of here and do something good. He wants to keep busy."

"Right, that's what I'll do: I'll keep him working and hopefully tire him out." I finished my coffee and then went over to see how Tom was.

Tom was getting better in colour, and he was his jolly self again. I told him what a fool he was for not letting us know, and to never let it happen again. He agreed, and said that Flo hadn't stopped nagging him about it. This was the first proper time I had spoken to Tom, so I asked what he did before retiring.

He was a policeman and worked his way up to chief inspector. He joined at eighteen and was finally forced to retire at sixty. He worked on a lot of cases; a friend even used him in a series of books. A film was made from one of them, but it wasn't big, and it flopped. He said he wished he could do more for the group; it just wasn't him to be infirm.

I asked his age, and he told me that he was seventy eight. Then I asked how he would feel about being a driver for the group. That way, there would always be someone in a car ready to take off in a hurry. He shook my hand and smiled, then said he would love to do that. It would remind him of the old days, and he was a great driver then. I said that once he was better, he could go out and do some practise with one of the other guys or myself. I'd done some escape and evasion driving in the army.

"That's something I've wanted to ask you, Nick," he said, looking through squinted eyes. "Those army days: which regiment were you in? You seem to know a lot for regular army."

I stared at him and smiled. He already knew the answer, but

wanted to hear it from the horse's mouth.

He smiled back, "Well?"

"I was in Twenty-Two Regiment down at Hereford for about twenty years. Made Sergeant Major before age got the better of me. I was stuck in the office most of the time, sorting the selection training. Got tired of the same things; wanted to go in the field, but I was getting slow. Still fit as a fiddle, but years of hard training does the body no good: aches and pains everywhere."

"What stuff have you done?" Tom's eyes started to shine; he was really interested in my history.

"Sorry, Tom, I just can't tell you, or I'd have to kill you ..." I started to laugh as he did, "One day I'll tell you, but not today, alright?"

"Alright, but I'll hold you to it."

I stood up and patted his shoulder. "If you feel up to it, I'll take you out tomorrow for a drive. *But* only if you're well; I will ask Flo first."

He shouted 'OK' after me, and I felt he would do his best to be fit the next day. People need to keep morale up, and by letting Tom do the driving I'd have extra men and women in the field.

Chapter Seven

"Dad, you should have seen us! We walked through about a hundred of them!" Jess and her group had just pulled in. She jumped out of the car and ran over to me covered in blood and guts and smelling of rotten corpse. Paul and Rachael walked over to us, smiling.

"We pulled up to the car park, and it was heaving with monsters. So Paul drove down the road a bit until we found one on its own. He killed it, and then we covered ourselves." She took a breath and looked back at her mother. "Then we drove back to the store and parked at the entrance. They started to walk over to us. I was really scared, but Paul told us to wait, and he got out and just stood there. They walked right by him, so he got a shopping trolley and pushed into some other trolleys, and the noise made them turn away. Then he told us to get out."

"That's right, mate," said Paul, shaking my hand when he reached me.

Rachael kissed me on the cheek. She turned to Jess and told her that they needed to wash first, then they could tell the rest of the story. Jess gave me a hug, and I gingerly hugged her back. They went away to wash in the moat.

The rest of us went to the car and started to empty it. The boot was full of tinned and dried food, as well as a load of medical supplies, with more pills for Tom and Josie. They also got magazines and books.

Just as we were finishing off, the second car pulled up. Once they were inside and the gates were closed, I could see something was wrong. There was a person missing: Marie.

"What happened?" I asked, pulling David's door open. His face was thunder.

"It's all my fault," he said in a whisper. "I should have made her wear the stuff."

Kelly and Steve climbed out of the car. I looked over to them, and they shook their heads. Steve asked Flo to take David away and get him something to drink.

Steve then told me their story. They reached the camping store easily. There was no trouble on the roads; they only saw a couple of the dead. On getting there, it all seemed quiet, so Steve and David checked out the store. Inside, there were about twenty of them wandering about, so they left and went in search of one to kill.

They got one, dragged it to the car, chopped it up and started to put it over themselves. Marie refused to do it, as it was so disgusting. So she was told to stay in the car. The rest entered the store and started to collect the supplies.

Whilst they were on the inside, more dead came wandering into the area. Tony thought that the car may have brought them in. When they came out with the supplies, Marie was starting to freak out. In a panic, she got out of the car, and that's when the swarm got her.

They killed most of the monsters, but it was too late for Marie. It was David who got them into the car and told Steve to drive away. All the way back, David was swearing and hitting the dash of the car. He started to calm down once they came close to the village, his anger vented, replaced by sadness.

"I'll tell you, Nick, it was frightening seeing her just get out like that. I couldn't believe David was so calm till we pulled off," Steve said, bowing his head. "We left the stuff there as well; we just dropped it to fight them things, and we had to get in the car. There were loads of good stuff as well, Kelly and me will go back."

"No," I said. "I'll go back with you, and we'll take Paul with us. Kelly can stay here, she looks worn out."

Kelly heard her name and came over, catching the end of the conversation. "Worn out, I'll do my bit," she said rather sharp. "Just because I'm a woman, you think you're better?" looking at me.

"Kelly, no, you look tired. I was just thinking of you, that's all. If you want to come, then come."

"I'm going."

"Right after lunch we'll go, OK?"

Everyone agreed.

Steve smiled and said, "No point washing then, hey?"

"No. See you in a bit." I walked over to Paul to tell him the news.

"Frigging hell, mate, I've just washed up. I'll be driver then."

We had lunch, and it was nice to get some good food down us. Whilst we were eating, Jess carried on with her story.

"The store was crawling with them," she started. "So we took our time collecting things, putting them into trolleys and taking them to the front doors. But we think the trolleys were making them aware of us, so we had to kill them. We left the stuff and just walked up to them, putting our weapons through their heads. You never told me how hard it was. Paul said to go through the temple, as it was the softest area on the head."

Paul nodded and agreed with her.

Jess carried on after taking a drink of coke, which she brought back. "It took us about half an hour till we got them all. Then we could shop till our hearts were content."

"Putting the stuff in the car was a pain," said Rachael. "We made a sort of chain and passed the things to each other. We thought it was a good way to stay unnoticed. Once full, we got back in the car and headed here."

"There's still a load of supplies there," said Paul, "as long as no one else takes them, it could work again."

Everyone agreed, but we needed to get the camping stuff – then get into the city. The longer we stayed at the castle, unprotected, the harder it was for us to defend it.

That afternoon we went to fetch the camping supplies. Most of the dead had gone by the time we got there, but we saw Marie. Paul put her out of her misery.

We got some good stuff for the camp. There were tents, groundsheets, torches and batteries, chemical toilets, sleeping bags, water filters and even a solar shower. Steve had his eyes on a generator, but I said to leave it, as it would make too much noise.

The journey back was uneventful, but once we pulled into the car park, I saw more of the dead. They must have known that we were there – all the more reason to get guns. At the gates were a couple of the monsters, so Steve and I got out and killed them. Once the gates opened, we ran inside as Paul drove in.

Chapter Eight

That night, we had our own tents to sleep in. I told the older ones to have the guard rooms, as they were drier and warmer. Not by much; but now we had better sleeping bags and ground sheets, they were the best places to spend the night. We had a hearty dinner cooked on gas stoves with proper pans.

The morale was still quite high, but you could sense apprehension about the coming morning, when some of us would be leaving. Hopefully, we'd only be gone for a couple of days. We made sure that there was plenty of wood for the fire, and I told Paul that no one was to leave the castle unless it was necessary. Also, I told him that if any dead neared, to kill them, as they need not attract even more attention.

The city was only about five miles away, but we didn't know what we'd face. What we did know was that after three miles the cordon would start. That would be the first obstacle to deal with. We set off early, just as the sun was rising, leaving David, as he was in no state to come. It was just Rachael and Jess with me in one car, and Kelly and Steve in the other.

Tom asked if he could be the driver for Kelly and Steve. I told him no. As I'd said before, there was the potential for a lot of walking, running and fighting. He said it was worth asking. I wished I could have taken him, but he was just too old, and I didn't want his death on my hands.

We headed towards Braunstone to get on the A47, which would take us straight into the city. We passed a lot of the dead on the roads, and the nearer we got, the more there were. We took it slow so we could check out places that we passed. I would stop the car, and we would arrange an RV (rendezvous). If we got split-up, we would meet at one of these places, starting with the nearest to the city.

Looking at some of the houses we passed, I swear I saw faces at the windows. Were they survivors or the dead just stuck in there? We didn't want to investigate yet, as we had no room for stragglers.

We came to the cordon on the Fosse Road, which ran from Braunstone, near the A5460, to the A50. It was about three-miles long, and we were at the part nearest to the city; it gave a run along its length. The cordon itself was heras fencing, stretching across the road and bolted to the houses at each side.

We sat in the car, just looking and assessing the situation. There were quite a lot of the dead about. Some had taken an interest in us, so we backed the cars away and went to the right until the dead had thinned out.

I saw a house with a door open and only two dead standing nearby. We stopped the cars, killed the two beasts, and grabbed our back packs and weapons. I had my knife belt and a machete; the others all carried knives too. Rachael carried the hedging tool that Paul had used before; Jess had my sword, and Steve and Kelly both had sharpened metal stakes.

We entered the house, shutting the door behind us, and checked to make sure it was clear. There were dead bodies in two of the upstairs rooms, both with the backs of their heads blown off. They had been there for quite some time – they were just dried-out husks. Looking out of a back window, I saw that this house backed onto another. That one had a back gate, which was open. That was our way into the city.

The others fetched the two dead in and started to chop

them up; we started to cover ourselves in the stuff. We then headed towards the back of the house; Kelly looked through the kitchen window and saw it was clear.

"Before we go: no talking, just use signs if you can, and if you need to talk, make sure none of them things hear you. And no rushing, it might attract them too. So, nice and steady," I said. "Now let's go."

I put my back against the fence, cupped my hand and lifted Jess up to peek over to see if the way was clear.

"Just one," she said, "I've got it," and over she went. There was a thud has she landed then a crunch as she killed the monster.

"All clear," she whispered.

I hoisted Rachael next, then Steve and Kelly. I jumped up and scrambled over, making quite a noise when I hit the ground. We waited a few minutes. Jess was at the gate looking out; she gave a thumbs up. Everything was clear, so we went into the street. I knew this area a little, as I had a friend who lived here when I was a kid. These streets were a maze of alleys, so I got my bearings and headed towards the city.

We came out on Tudor Road which joined the A47 and A5460. This was a famous area: the remains of King Richard III were supposedly discarded from the bridge that crossed the river and canal. But he was found in a car park in the city some years ago.

The few dead we saw we left alone, and they us. When we came out on to the main road, we stood facing the Holiday Inn. We could see that there were a lot of dead milling around, so we walked around them and headed on to the High Street. We started our way through the centre.

There were dead husks everywhere; there must have been one hell of a battle here. I was looking out for dead soldiers, as I wanted their weapons. The few we found were ripped to pieces with no sign of the guns. From the look of the affected, the military finally realised they had to go for the head.

We carried on through the centre of the city, keeping an eye out for living as well as dead. There were plenty of the latter. We walked up Granby Street, then we turned left on to St George's way. I saw a flash of light up in the retail park to our right, and then I thought I saw movement. I halted the group and pointed up to where I saw the flash. Everyone looked where I told them to, and then back at me. I called them together and told them what I saw.

"Are you sure?" asked Steve.

"Yes, I'm positive," I answered back. "The entrance is just ahead, let's take a look."

As we approached the road leading to the retail park, there were about a hundred of the dead milling around. As we got closer, I saw that the road was blocked with cars side-to-side and bumper-to-bumper. I counted five deep. I then saw a group of people watching us from the top of a hill. Some of them were pointing our way. I'm sure I could hear them talking. I looked at my group – they had seen. They then looked at me. I pointed away from the monsters so that we could regroup and talk.

"Should we try and reach them?" asked Rachael.

"I'm not sure," I said. "They may be dangerous, plus I would rather do it on my terms."

"I agree," said Steve. "There might be more of them up there, hiding, and I don't fancy being attacked."

"They could be friendly," Jess intervened. "They may only be survivors like us; they must have fought hard to stay alive here."

"That's right," I was firm, "all the more to keep us away.

They don't know who we are."

Just then, one of the dead turned towards us, then another – then even more.

"Let's get away before they all come," I urged.

We started off, but they were following us. We picked up the pace, but more of them were attracted by now. We were up a creek. So we ran – this seemed to agitate them. Before we knew it, they were coming from every direction.

I knew the T.A. Centre was just past a group of factories, but there was no way through. We'd have to take the road. I ran up to a couple of monsters and stabbed them in the head; I could hear the others doing the same. I shouted to make sure my group was following me. As I turned, I could see Jess swinging the sword, taking heads off – I felt so proud of her.

Steve was fighting back-to-back with Kelly. They were taking them down by the dozen. Rachael was struggling with one, trying to push it away from her as it tried to gnash at her neck. She dropped the hedging tool in the struggle. I could see two were at her back, so I ran, pulling my machete from my belt. I swung, taking the top of the head off one, and with the other hand I plunged my knife into the second creature's eye.

I turned to Rachael and helped with the one trying to bite her. She pulled the knife from her belt and stabbed it in the side of the head. Stopping to swoop-up the hedging tool, she gave me a kiss, and we ran to help the others.

We must have taken down at least twenty, but they were still coming. We were moving slowly backwards, towards our goal, but it was still a long way off.

I saw a pub about thirty metres away, and I shouted to my group to try and make it there. The others all nodded and trudged along. By the time we got there, another twenty or more were down. I was starting to lose my strength, and I could see the others flagging. We made it to the pub and shut the doors when we were all inside.

I told Steve to find something to put through the door handles. He smashed a chair and put the leg through – it only just held. Whilst I was securing the doors, I told the girls to make sure the building was safe. Then I told Steve to find something to lash the doors together. He found some rope and came running – the doors were starting to give with the hoard of dead pressing outside. He put the rope through and wound it round until it was secure. I slumped against the doors. I could still feel them pushing, but it was holding now. Kelly and the girls came back: they found some in the back and upstairs, but dealt with them. We all sat down, worn out. I asked if everyone was okay and if anyone was bit.

"Just knackered," said Steve, "how come they came after us?"

I shook my head, the gore suits had failed us somehow. "Not sure why, as we wasn't too loud when we were talking. I think they knew we wasn't one of them."

"Dad, I was sweating with all the walking. Maybe it was that they smelt?" Jess offered.

"We all were ... so yes, it could be that. We'll have to make sure in future to redo the guts once in a while."

Jess and Rachael went looking for food and drinks; we didn't want to use ours just in case we'd need it later. They found bottles of juice, a couple of boxes of crisps, a tin of beans and peas.

"Better than nothing," smiled Kelly, opening a pack of cheese and onion and swigging back a juice.

We all ate and drank our fill. I told the group that we should stay put until the morning – no point until then, with all the dead outside. Jess suggested we get the dead they killed, chop them up, and put it over the doors and windows. She thought it might mask us. Everyone thought it was a great idea.

We then went around the pub making it secure, so we could sleep in peace. We got bedding down from upstairs – we were going to sleep in the bar. I didn't want to be away from the door, just in case.

Chapter Nine

We woke the next morning to the sound of rain. I went over to the window and peered out; it was throwing it down. Most of the dead had gone, but there were still quite a few out there. Rachael came over to me, put her arm around my waist and looked out.

"Nice day for ducks," she said.

"Yeah, don't seem to bother them," I replied, nodding towards the dead outside. "I don't think the gut suit will be any good in this anyway."

From behind me, Steve said, "Too right, as soon as we put it on, the rain will just wash it off."

Jess and Kelly were now at the window looking out too.

"Let's get away from the window before they see us," I ordered, and they moved.

"How far to go?" asked Kelly.

"This gets my goat; it's just round the corner, less than half a mile," I said.

"Could we make a run for it?" Steve wondered.

"Maybe, if there's not too many of them, but we don't know what the T.A. Centre's like. It could be overrun or empty. I would like to be covered in guts to be on the safe side," I said, thoughtfully. "That way, we can walk in and assess the situation first."

"Makes sense," agreed Kelly.

Rachael said, "So we may as well stay here till the rain stops."

"Yes," I answered, "let's just get comfortable and wait the rain out."

I sat in one of the bedroom windows, watching the dead walking and hanging about. This was the first time I actually studied and thought deeper about them. How did this virus contaminate us? And how did it revive the dead? How much of the real person was left? Did they know what they were doing?

Was there a place where people knew about this virus? Was it man made or natural? I felt it must be the former. During my time in the forces, I was trained on NBC warfare. NBC stood for nuclear, biological and chemical. I needed to know how to act if anything like this ever happened. In some Middle Eastern counties, despots would gas their own people, so it was always a threat. In the First Gulf War, a lot of personnel were given injections to combat a multitude of threats. Saddam gassed the Kurds in northern Iraq; luckily it never came to that with us.

I wondered if they had tried some new agent in Africa – was it worse than they thought, did it just get out of control? In London the government might still have facilities and people trying to find a cure. After this thought, I wanted to go to London and find out. The Ministry of Defence would hold some answers, and I knew how to get in. I had been part of a COBRA team when terrorist threats were on. I would talk to Rachael, after we got weapons and made safe the castle. I would only take people who wanted to come.

Night started to fall, and the rain slowed right down. If it had stopped in the morning we'd move out. If not, I might just go on recce to see what was about – we couldn't stay here too long.

The next morning was just as bad as the day before; the rain was so heavy that it bounced off the tarmac. The dead were still hanging around, but in fewer numbers. Could we make a break with only a small number out there? I went from one window to another upstairs, trying to see how many there were. I counted fifteen: yes we could. The pub was on the corner of a junction, so

I could see down most of both roads, and there were only one or two infected about. It was the T.A. Centre I was worried about. It may have been used as a barracks for the forces that guarded the city after the outbreak. Maybe the soldiers got infected and stuck inside the compound and buildings.

We had a breakfast of crisps and pop, sorted out our back-packs, got our weapons ready or stored for quick access, and off we went. Despite the rain, we opted to push forward to the centre. Leaving by the back door and into the pub yard, Steve opened the gate. The rest of us ran to the nearest roamers and killed them. I took the lead with Rachael, then came Jess and Kelly. Steve brought up the rear. We ran the whole way to the centre, killing the few dead that we encountered.

Once at the centre, I stopped the group and peered round the fence into the grounds of the compound. The fence was the new anti-climb type where you couldn't get a foothold, and it was two-metres tall. It was just as I feared: the place was crawling with the dead.

I could see guns lying on the floor about the grounds; *were their magazines full?* If so, we could simply shoot a lot of the dead at a distance. I backed us off before any of the roamers could see us. I told Steve to check over the fence. With my back to the wooden wall, I cupped my fingers and boosted Steve up.

He peered over and said, "Clear," quietly. I heaved him up and over, then went Kelly, Rachael, Jess and finally me.

We sat in silence for a few moments. I was looking around the yard we were in, thinking up a plan of action. The others were just looking at me, waiting for me to speak.

"Right," I started, "here's the plan. Over this fence are loads of roamers. If we go in and fight them hand-to-hand we'll be overrun in minutes."

My group agreed.

"Over there," I pointed to a low roofed building with a flat top, "is a good vantage point to take out the dead with guns."

There was a hush as the group thought about what I just said.

"Before that, two of us will jump over this fence and collect as many guns as we can and then jump back over." I paused. "I want a platform built on this side, so that we can pull you back quick." I looked around the group. "I want two of the lightest to go over, so that's you Rachael …"

"I'll go with her," said Kelly, before I could say Jess' name.

I looked at her and thanked her with a nod.

I carried on, "When you're over, the first gun you find, throw it back to me, and I'll cover you both. Don't waste time getting your arms full; just grab the nearest and get back. Once you're in there, they will be over you in a flash."

We started to build the platform using barrels and planks, making it wide enough to hold us all. The rain was stopping, thankfully. Unfortunately, the noise we made attracted some of the dead, so I sent Steve and Jess farther down the fence to bang and make a noise, hoping to pull the roamers away.

Kelly and Rachael climbed onto the platform and crouched down, hiding. I signalled a thumbs-up to Steve and Jess, and they started to make a noise. Kelly popped her head over and watched the roamers moving away; she touched Rachael's shoulder, and then both were over. I jumped up and waited for the gun. Kelly was back, handing me one in seconds.

I quickly checked the magazine: there was a slit in the side so you could see the rounds. It was half full; I half-cocked it to see if there was a round in the spout – there was. I pushed it back and was aiming at the nearest dead – it was less than two seconds since I was handed the gun.

The roamer was moving towards them, so I fired and caught it in the chest. My aim was low, so I adjusted and got it through the head. I took out six more before I saw the girls making their way back. I called to the others, and they climbed the platform ready to take the weapons and pull them over.

I took out another five or so, and the rest were starting to make their way over to us. There must have been about a hundred of them. I emptied the magazine into the throng and then jumped down, taking deep breaths to calm down after the adrenaline rush. It was less than three minutes since we started.

The girls had collected eight rifles in all – nine, including the one I'd been using. I took out the magazines and ejected the bullets in the barrels. Some were full, others half or less. Each mag will hold 32 rounds. I emptied all the magazines into a plastic bag and told Jess to wipe them down and count them. I then handed the magazine cases to the others, and told them to clean them down as best they could, trying not to get any dust or water into them. I then started to strip down five of the rifles, and gave them a good clean. I tore my tee shirt into strips to clean the barrels and breaches. After a little scout around the yard, I found some engine oil. It was a little thick for guns, but as long as I didn't put too much in they would be fine.

Once I'd finished, I asked Jess how many rounds there were. She told me 166. I never liked to fill a magazine to the top – sometimes, if the spring was pushed too much, it could jam. I showed the group how to fill the magazines, just inserting thirty into each one. This gave us five full magazines and one with sixteen.

While they were loading, I could hear the dead on the other side of the fence, scratching and pushing at it. I just hoped it held while we were sorting ourselves out. Once the magazines were filled, I showed them how to use the rifles, setting them to single burst so no bullets were wasted. With the half-full magazine, we sighted-in with a target I'd put on the fence – I put it at head height, hoping one or two might get hit behind. Each person had four rounds. I gave each person a gun. With the first two rounds, I checked the sights, then the last two were used to make sure the sights were right for that person.

I climbed onto the platform and looked into the grounds: there were now about 150 dead roaming in the yard, brought out by the sound of the gun fire. I could see cars and military vehicles, including land rovers, lorries and even an APC (Armoured Personal Carrier). I liked the look of the APC – it carried its own .50-cal machine gun. Even the lorries had machine guns mounted to their roofs. But first we had to get rid of the roaming dead.

I jumped back down and laid out a new plan. Jess, Rachael, Kelly and Steve were to stand on the platform and kill the dead at the fence. All they needed to do was to stab them in the heads from above. Jess had my sword; the others could use steel stakes. I would lay on the roof of the hut and take down the ones farther out. I had five full mags, so I'd take out quite a lot of them.

The guys climbed onto the platform and looked over the side – the dead started to go into a frenzy. The fence started to bow inward with the surge of activity. Straight away, they plunged their weapons down, brains flying everywhere. The dead just kept on coming, all lining up to die. I climbed up to the flat roof, got into a good position and started to fire into the crowd, putting bullets into their heads. Again, the noise brought more out; by that point, most of the buildings were emptying. I could hear the dead groaning and hissing at the fence and the crunch and squelch of heads being stabbed.

As I loaded my second mag, I quickly looked over at the group: the bodies must have started to pile up. Some of the roamer's heads reached the top of the fence. I started to lay down fire near the fence to help the others from getting overwhelmed.

I was on my fourth mag when I looked at my group again. The

surge seemed to be slowing down; the mound of dead stopped the roamers from getting to the fence. One or two climbed the pile, but the group soon took them down.

I was still shooting the dead when, half-way through my last mag, there seemed to be no more to kill. I stood up, and looked into the centre. It was a slaughter house – blood and bodies everywhere. I climbed down and the group stayed where they were just looking down at their pile of bodies.

As I got to them, Kelly said, "So much death ..." It was just a statement; we all thought about it while getting our breath back.

"Right," I said, "over we go, collect more magazines, and load your rifles. Be ready for more, keep your eyes and ears peeled."

I took the lead with Jess, Kelly, Rachael, and Steve bringing up the rear. As we passed rifles, we picked up the mags and pocketed them.

The centre comprised of three buildings. At the front, the main building, with the drill hall, mess, offices and stores. Behind that, running parallel, was the platoon building where each platoon would have its own stores. Then, to our right was the vehicle garage and workshop.

We came to the corner of the main building and I signalled everyone to the wall. I looked round the corner and saw the main gates. Like the fence, they were two-metres high and made of thick steel; best of all, they were closed. The dead were trying to get in.

We moved around the corner, hugging the wall. When we got to the next corner, I looked around it: there were two roamers standing at a door half-way down the building. I whispered that I would take them out with my knife, told my group to wait, and I was off.

I ran up to them, killed the first going through the temple, and as the second turned, I pushed my knife up through its chin and into the brain. It fell. I ran back to the corner of the main building and waved the others over. Peering around the corner, I couldn't see the door that led into the drill hall. Slowly, we moved round, and there was another one, it seemed to be standing guard. I showed myself; it came at me, and I pushed the knife into its forehead – it fell.

Just inside the door on the left was a store for the quartermaster. I knew that keys would be in there, but first I wanted to make sure the building was clear. This room was empty; I shut the door.

The next door was the armoury; again, we cleared it and shut the door. Then we were in the main drill hall. Along the left wall were more storerooms for platoons, and over to the right was a door leading to the offices. We cleared the left side first, shutting the doors after us. At the end was the door leading to the messes, but we went over to the other side of the hall to clear the offices first.

Once this was done, we made our way around the building. The mess downstairs was the normal soldiers' mess; upstairs was the sergeants' and officers' mess. There were also a few bedrooms, for when people stayed overnight. After an hour, we cleared the whole building – we only found two dead, in the bedrooms.

Once the building was cleared, we went to the kitchen to see what food there was. There was an abundance of tinned food, so we tucked into a good feast, even if it was cold. We also sorted out bedrooms: we could have a good night's sleep, as we felt safe and secure for the first time in months.

Chapter Ten

The next morning, we started to look around the building for supplies and weapons. We found the keys to the armoury and went to have a look. It was just as I thought: plenty of pistols and rifles – there were even a couple of top-of-the-range sniper rifles. I felt giddy, like a kid in a sweet shop. There was loads of ammunition. I picked up a pistol, checked it and found some clips (magazines) for it. I then loaded up and found a holster. I took that and put it on; it had pouches for the clips, so I filled them. The others started to load themselves with weapons. That's when I stopped them.

"We'll take enough for everyone, but no one uses them until I've trained you. I don't want accidents," I said.

"Will you train us now, dad?" asked Jess.

"I will later – I don't want to shoot any weapons yet. We need the roamers outside to go away so we can check the other buildings. Plus, when we've got everything we need, we'll have to make a break for it," I explained, to the group's displeasure. "OK, you can use your rifles from earlier. Fill yourselves with ammo now, and keep them on single shot." It was a compromise.

We piled the ammo boxes and weapons into the hall. There were enough weapons for everyone back at the castle, plus more. I made sure we had gun oil and rolls of gun-cleaning material. Once this was done we went to the kitchen and gathered all the food. We also found a pallet full of army rations which would last for years. We found packing crates to help us. I put three aside and loaded them with a couple of pistols and some ammunition.

"What's that for?" asked Steve.

"We'll drop this off at the retail park when we pass, it might help them," I said and carried on filling them.

"Why, they didn't help us?" he replied.

"What could they have done?"

"Nothing, right?"

"Right, let's finish here then go over and check the vehicles."

We all carried on working – it was tiring. Two-hours later we had what we could and took a break.

There were two doors into the main building: one at the side, which we entered by, and the main door, which was half-way down the back. We left by the latter, as we didn't want to attract the attention of the dead at the main gate. We didn't bother with the platoon building; we had all we needed.

We made our way around the back to the APC. The keys were in it, and it started first time. Was I glad the army looked after their transport – the fuel gauge was full. Next, we went to one of the lorries that had a roof-mounted machine gun. Again, the keys were in it, and the tank was full. Both vehicles ran on diesel, so we went into the workshop and found five-gallon jerrycans. We also found a siphon, so we next started to fill as many cans as we could and put them into the lorry. We then moved the APC, backing it up to the drill-hall doors, and loaded the ammo and weapons into it. Then we did a switch around with the lorry and loaded the rest of the stuff onto it.

The noise of the two vehicles started to bring roamers in again, and they were getting rather agitated. We put the two vehicles into position in front of the gates, ready for a quick take off in the morning. I wasn't going to risk a night move:

all we'd have were headlights. We agreed that daylight would be better.

As we sat in the officers' mess, drinking spirits, we chatted about how good it felt to be armed and ready for anything. Jess was missing Neave, as were Rachael and I. We hoped the castle was OK, but I trusted Paul, David and Tony to keep it safe. It was hard to believe we'd only been away for four days – it felt like weeks. We all turned in, ready for an early start.

Chapter Eleven

The day was bright when we looked out the window to see how many roamers were about. A lot had wandered off during the night. After a nice, cold breakfast, I took Kelly out to show her how to use the machine gun on the roof of the lorry. Steve was going to drive it and she was going to be gunner. She took it all in very quickly. When I asked her to talk me through it, she was very good.

Next was Jess's turn on the .50 cal. She was also very competent with the big gun. Rachael had the worst job: she would have to open the gates, which would take time, as they would be very heavy. We stood at the gates and tried to kill as many as we could, using steel stakes through the gaps. There were only about twenty; we killed them all easily, but I told Rachael to keep her knife ready for any loose ones. If push came to shove, we'd use the guns, but I didn't want to attract any more, as the vehicles would make enough noise.

We jumped in, and once the gates were open we started the engines. It was just as if two dragons had roared to life. We drove through quickly. I stopped and jumped out to give Rachael backup. I ran to one gate as she was closing the other – it only seemed right to shut them. I heard a shot fired, then another; the roamers must be starting to come out. We finally shut the gates and ran back to the APC. I took out my pistol and shot two that were at the rear of the lorry. Rachael ran around to the passenger side of our ride and climbed in. More dead were coming out again, drawn by the gunfire. I killed three more before getting in the APC. I shut the door, looked over at Rachael, smiled at her and started to move off.

The APC was slow but powerful. I just ran into any dead that were in my way. I could feel them going under the wheels. Turning left, and then motoring up the road, we reached the junction with the pub we stayed in. We could have turned right: It would have been quicker to get home, but I wanted to drop off the package for the people at the retail centre.

It only took a couple of minutes to get there. As we came to the traffic island, I could see about twenty dead standing around. When they heard the big vehicles, they turned and came towards us. I shouted at Jess to take them out – I forgot how loud the gun was. Then I heard Kelly doing the same from the lorry. Within seconds they were all down.

Stopping by the piled-up cars, I jumped out and went to the back of the lorry. Steve and Rachael covered me while I pulled the boxes out and put it down on the road. I looked up and saw a crowd of people up at the top. I waved and ran back to the APC. Steve let off a few rounds as roamers started to appear. Everyone safe in their transport, we headed off back to the castle.

The journey back was uneventful. Any dead in front of me went under the wheels. There seemed more of them on the way out than on the way in. When we came to the heras fencing, I put my foot down to pick up speed, crashing through. The fencing went flying and landed on the ground. Steve drove the lorry over it and kept moving.

It took us half an hour to get back. As we came down the hill, before you got to Kirby Muxloe, I looked over at the castle and saw smoke from the bonfire – it looked serene. I must admit, I was worried for them with half the group gone, and I couldn't wait to see Neave again.

As we pulled into the castle car park, I saw people on the top of the building. They started to wave: Jess and Kelly must have been waving at them. Then the gate opened and they all came running out. In front was Paul carrying Neave. We turned our rides and backed them up to the moat bridge. I didn't want to take them over yet; it might not take the weight.

Just as I stopped and switched off the engine, Jess slid down the front of the APC and ran to her daughter, giving her massive hugs. Rachael and I were soon with them, hugging and crying with happiness.

"Bloody hell, mate," said Paul, "looks like you had a good shopping trip!"

Steve and Kelly walked up, hand in hand, with smiles on their faces. They shook hands and had their backs patted. Everyone was glad we were back. When I broke from the crowd, I noticed three new faces standing at the gates, and one missing.

"Where's David, and who are they?" I asked Paul, pulling him away from the group.

"That's a story for later, after you've told us yours," he said with a grin like the Cheshire Cat.

Everyone, including the new faces, unloaded the lorry and APC. There was a lot of oohing and hawing as things were taken off. The guns caught more interest than most things; we put them all under cover in Tom and Flo's sleeping space. They would have to be moved out.

Once everything was stowed away, Josie came over with a hot cup of tea. It was nectar after four days of cold food and drink. We all went for a wash in the moat. When we had finished, we felt nearly human again, but I would miss the bed at the T.A. Centre.

After a hot meal, we told the group our story, and about the people at the retail park. We also mentioned the possibility of other survivors in the houses we saw on the way there.

"The centre seems a safe place," said Tony, "why don't we move there? It's better than sleeping outside, and we do have winter coming soon."

The group were agreeing, to have proper beds and a roof would be good. Plus the fencing kept the dead out. I must admit, it sounded good, but I had my own plans.

"So what's their story, and where is David?" I asked, nodding at the three newbies who had not said anything yet.

It was on the afternoon that we left that they had turned up. The three people, two women and a man, lived in the village, just off the main street. There were six of them in a house when it had all started; they had kept themselves hidden since the outbreak. After a few weeks, the dead started to arrive, and, of course, before they knew it, the whole village was overrun.

They had seen us coming and going, and fighting the roamers, so they thought they would chance coming out and finding us. They saw the smoke from the castle and started to make their way. Before they got down the first road, the dead were after them. They ran for their lives, but there were so many dead: three of them were killed. The people had armed themselves with bats and spades, but the dead didn't stop when they were hit – they just got back up.

It wasn't until they got to the castle that Paul, Tony, Jayne and David went out to help them. David was on guard and saw them running into the car park with the hoard on their backs. He called down, and when he saw the problem, gathered the others for help. Paul took at least half a dozen down, as did David. Tony killed about two or three, and Jayne led the newcomers into the castle. Once safe, the others retreated and shut the gates behind them.

They spent the next couple of hours killing the dead with stakes, through the gate. Even the old ones helped with the deed; every hand was needed. Only when the dead finally stopped coming did my group ask who they were.

The man's name was Nathan, and his wife was Rachael. (That was going to get confusing, I'd said.) The other woman was Emily, Rachael's cousin.

The next day they spent moving the affected bodies to the farm. It rained like mad that day, and they had to keep applying the guts so the dead wouldn't smell them. It took most of the day to transport them, and they had to kill one or two more while they did it.

The next day, David wanted to go and find other survivors and bring them back. His reasoning was that they needed more numbers, just in case we didn't come back. He hadn't been seen since. Paul, Tony, and Nathan went out a couple of times to find him but didn't. Then again, they didn't travel too far away: it was too dangerous.

"Right, tomorrow I'm taking you out," I pointed at Paul, Tony and Jayne, "and we're going to do some gun training. I need everyone to know how to use them."

"What about this?" said Paul, holding his hook up.

"We'll work round that," I said, smiling.

Nathan spoke for the first time since we came back, "How about us?"

"I don't know you, and I'm not giving you a gun until I do. You could be an advance party sent to attack us for all I know."

"Nick, they have been helpful and kind since they arrived here," said Flo.

"Remember what happened back home," I stated, a little too harshly.

"Yes, but we've seen no one at all."

"I'll take them out to see if we can find David tomorrow afternoon. If they prove themselves, we'll see."

"Right, alright then," she said, a little quietly.

I wasn't going to mention going to London yet, but going back to the T.A. Centre could be a way forward. Yes, it had beds. Yes, it was safe and secure. But it was surrounded by a lot of the dead. The trip back could be dangerous as well. Maybe going out and finding a lonely farm, or house in the middle of nowhere, was the answer: a place that we could defend if we needed to. I tried to think of somewhere, but couldn't. I was tired and wanted my bed.

I put Tony on guard, to be taken over by Paul later. Nathan offered to do a shift. I said no, not tonight. Tom and Flo were sharing with Josie in a tent we put up for them. I made sure they had enough warm sleeping bags and blankets. With that, we all said good night and turned in.

Chapter Twelve

We decided to leave the lorry and APC outside the castle walls. Room was being taken up fast with the new additions, and more were to come, possibly. Plus, using the dry guard rooms for stores, the flat grass was getting crowded with tents and people. A new home would be a good idea.

I was planning a training session the next morning, one outside of the castle. No way was I going to fire guns around here. I would do it in the back of beyond. At the same time, I would look for somewhere to live; London may have to wait. Whilst having a nice, warm breakfast, I was trying to think where to go and train. I remembered a quarry out at Markfield which was high and fenced, with only two entrances for the public to walk through. I finalised my plans, we would go there.

We took one of the cars and loaded it with a rifle and pistol for each person. Once I'd trained these people, these would be their personal weapons – they had to learn to look after them. I placed Nathan and Kelly on guard (telling Kelly to keep an eye on Nathan, and let me know how he worked). Kelly had her rifle and spare mags. I put the rest of the girls on cleaning duties and wanted reports when I got back.

Travelling to the quarry was a great journey; Paul seemed to be his old shelf, laughing and chatting. He was looking forward to firing the guns – he'd never shot one before, neither had Tony or Jayne. We met a few roamers in a village called Ratby, which was Kirby's neighbour, just two miles away, but we drove by them. As we came to the far edge of Ratby, we turned left for Markfield. This road was about three miles in length. Halfway along were two farms next to each other. The land around was flat and open. I pointed and said we'd have to check it out as a possible place to stay for the winter.

Turning right at the end of the road there was a row of houses. I could see windows smashed and even saw roamers inside. We passed a dog kennels and stopped. I had a quick look, and then backed up for a better view. I drove into the grounds. To our right were a house and what looked like stables. We drove into the car park and did a slow 180-degree turn. I saw a dead horse's half-eaten carcass. A large group of dead were on a narrow road leading to another car park, so we left. I thought it could have been a good home, but there seemed to be no way to protect it.

I turned left, back onto the road, and made another left. We passed a school on our right that was full of dead children. I stopped the car and we silently watched. Jayne started to cry – these were the first child roamers we'd seen. I drove on, feeling sick; we all stayed quiet until we came to the quarry.

Opening the boot of the car, I gave everyone a rifle and a pistol. I took a box of ammunition out and we walked to the quarry. I had my machete in hand just in case we came across a roamer. There were none. I sat everyone down in a clearing and went to check the other exit. It was clear, we were alone.

I first talked about weapon safety and husbandry, including how and when to keep it clean. If you hadn't used it, it should be cleaned every night; if you had, as soon possible. A clean and looked-after weapon looks after you, I told them. Next we filled the magazines. The rifles took 5.56mm rounds, and the pistols were 9mm. Then we zeroed the weapon to each person. After each burst of fire, we would wait for ten minutes to make sure it had not attracted any of the dead.

Next we did target practice. I only gave them one full mag each, as I didn't want to waste any. Once everyone was comfortable with their weapons, I told them they were never to leave their side. With each of the pistols, there was a holster. I told them that these were to stay on their belts at all times.

We had just started to pack away when we heard movement in the bushes. Guns were pointed to the area of the noise; I whispered to lower the weapons. The noise stopped, I went over to the bushes. A fox ran out, and I heard a shot from behind me. As I turned, Paul was laying on the floor, blood all around him. I thought the worst: he was dead. Jayne held the smoking gun with fear and shock on her face. The fox made her jump, and she had her finger on the trigger – she had fired. Paul was saying something, he was trying to get up. I ran over to him and drew my knife. When I reached him, he was on his knees, holding his arm.

"Who the fuck shot me?" he spat through gritted teeth.

I ripped his shirt open and saw that the bullet had gone right through. It must have nicked an artery to be bleeding so much. I pulled a handkerchief from my pocket and plugged the hole.

"Back to the car, quick: we need the first aid kit!"

Jayne kept on apologizing, saying it made her jump; she thought it was a roamer. I told her he'd be okay. I also told Tony to take the gun off her and have her carry the ammo box.

Back at the car was a roamer. I called to Tony to deal with it. I heard the shot and the back of its head was gone. I lowered Paul to the ground, with his back to the car, and opened the boot. Tony stood guard while Jayne stored the ammo; she was crying and still saying sorry to Paul.

He looked her in the eyes, smiled and kissed her forehead: "Don't worry, pet, at least you didn't kill me. Just do as Nick says: keep that trigger clear till you're sure, alright?"

She kissed his cheek, nodded and got up. She went to the boot, took her gun and stood guard while I finished the first aid. Hole all cleaned, compressed and covered, Paul got up, wincing when he used his arm.

"Just hope the next time she doesn't get me," he laughed as we all climbed into the car.

"You're one lucky man," I said, as I turned the car around and headed back down the hill.

On entering Markfield, we were stopped by a hoard of the monsters. The road was blocked by them, and I could see no way through. I put the car in reverse and did a J-turn, driving back the way we had just come. I looked into my rear-view mirror: they were coming after us, but we were gone. They would never catch a speeding car. I had to think of another route back to the castle. We would have to go via Thornton, Botcheston, Desford and back into Kirby Muxloe. It was one hell of a long way round, but I couldn't risk going through Markfield again.

As always, we saw dead roaming around. We just drove past, no point stopping to kill them. We would only attract more, so we kept on going.

Paul getting shot made me ponder my decision to arm the group. Would there be any more accidents? I would have to drill weapon safety into them – they must understand how easy it was to kill someone by accident. I looked in the mirror and saw that Jayne's eyes were still very red, but I could see her steel resolve. She had learnt her lesson the hard way. I just hoped that no one else had to do the same. Maybe Jayne's story would make the others think before pulling the trigger.

As the castle came into view, I looked over and stopped the car. We all got out: in the castle car park was a crowd of people. They were shouting and screaming at the occupants. Some had climbed onto the APC and lorry. I was so glad I took the machine gun and .50 cal off them.

At the top of the castle, I could just make out Steve and Kelly, with their rifle aimed at the crowd. I saw Steve jerk, then heard the shot he fired. The crowd went quiet and backed off a little. The people on the vehicles jumped down and used them for cover. I could hear Steve shouting something but couldn't make it out.

We loaded ourselves up; Paul could only use his pistol, so I made him stay at the back to keep an eye out for roamers. The noise and gunfire would surely attract them. I told my group to use knifes on any dead they saw. I wanted to flank the group without them knowing.

Walking down the main road, we saw a group of roamers, so we attacked them with knifes, killing them all. We could see some further down, so I told Paul to wait there and stop them coming after us. The rest of us carried on down the side road leading to the castle. There were a few more dead roamers. Parked up were four minibuses. There was no one with them.

We took our time getting to the car park, as we didn't want the interlopers to see us till the last second. I could see Steve and Kelly clearly on the turrets, and at the gate I could see the rest of our group. Tom was at the front, talking to someone. That's when I saw David, tied and gagged.

"You cannot come in. We haven't the room or the food. Please leave him here, and go on your way," I heard Tom pleading.

"Just let us in, old man, or he dies now," the man held a knife to David's throat.

David was shaking his head, telling Tom not to let them in.

"We want your food and now your guns," said the man,

"then we'll leave you be."

A tap on my shoulder made me turn from the scene in front of me, it was Paul.

"There's a load of them bastards on the way, I got a few, but there were too many so I pegged it here."

From bad to worse: roamers behind, people wanting us dead in front. *Should we hide or make a stand?*

"Gut suits," I said, "find the nearest one."

We looked around; there was one up the road, near the minibuses. The roamers were nearly on us as we got to it. I checked a bus and it was open, we all dived in quick. The first ones must have seen us; they started to hit the sides of the bus and tried to push in the windows. I heard another shot ring out, and the roamers turned towards the noise. They started ambling toward the castle.

Looking out of the window, I could see Steve aiming at the dead, but he was missing them. Then I realised what he was doing. He must have seen us – he was drawing the roamers away and towards the group.

We all watched the roamers heading towards the crowd. A couple of them turned and started to shout and point. The roamers were just metres away from them and starting to speed up. They grabbed the first in the crowd, pulling and biting.

A large man wielding an axe strode towards the dead and took out three in a massive swing, but on the backstroke, one grabbed his arm, taking a bite. The man screamed as two others brought him down, starting on his stomach. Before long, more affected had bundled him, intent on a meal. Other roamers walked around the dining group, plunging randomly into the crowd.

Some people started to run away, while others stood and fought. Dead were dropping, but there were too many of them.

I think the whole village of the dead had come to dine on the newly arrived group. People had their limbs pulled off; the dead eating them like you would a chicken leg, just standing there munching away.

There was no gunfire – the castle, with its strong gates, would hold. I knew David would be part of the feeding frenzy. He was tied and would not be able to defend himself. Some of the people dived into the moat and swam to the inner shore. *Would our people help them or push them back?*

Kelly disappeared from the turret; Steve was still watching the riot below. A woman was being pulled apart by a group of dead. She was screaming as more roamers joined in. You could hear her over the general din. As her legs and arms gave way, her torso fell to the floor, and roamers covered it in quick time.

One was walking towards us carrying a head in its hand, fingers in the eye sockets. In the other hand it held what looked like a large string of sausages. I soon realised they were intestines.

We felt helpless watching the carnage going on in front of us, but what could we do? These people had threatened our group, but did they deserve what they got? Maybe some of them did, but others may have simply followed to feel safe within a strong group. They must have been strong to survive as long as they had, but at what cost?

There must have been a couple of hundred dead out there. Most of the living had either turned roamer or ran off. There was no way we could take on that lot and get safely back into the castle. The dead now started towards the gates, knowing that there was more food inside. But our people would be safe, I was sure of that.

We got out of the bus and started to dismember the dead roamer near us, covering ourselves in it. We walked back the way we came; I looked up to the turret and saw Steve waving. He had the same thought as us: we were going to walk round to the farm next door, climb through the hedge and swim across the moat. I gave the thumbs up, and carried on walking to catch the others up.

I saw a couple of people running off down the old Kirby Road, which used to link Glenfield with Kirby Muxloe. We left them alone. When we got to the farm, three men came out of a barn and stood facing us, ready to attack.

"You're not geeks," one said, moving towards us. They looked angry and dangerous.

"No," I said, and we all raised our weapons at the same time. "We're not, but you can be if you want."

"No man, no, I want to live, and get away from them things." We'd scared them; they set down their weapons. "Who are you people?" he asked, "and where did you get the guns?"

"Not your problem, unless you start trouble. Get out of here, and don't come back."

They walked around us and ran off. I silently wished them luck. Could we have helped them, or would they have turned on us? I didn't know, but my gut feeling told me the latter.

We could see the back side of the castle. I could see Kelly and Jess pointing their guns at a small group of people who made it across the moat. Nathan also stood with her, he had Jess's sword. I called out and told them that it was us, and that we'd be swimming across.

I had to help Paul across, with his bad arm he was struggling to swim. The strangers were now sitting on the grass, on a corner of the castle's land. With water on two sides it was easy to guard. I went over to Tom, not looking at the prisoners, and asked him what happened.

They had turned up about an hour ago. Tom spotted the

minibuses as they turned into the side road. They must have come in from the opposite end of the village; they didn't come in the way we did.

Their leader dragged David out of the first bus and pushed him towards the castle. There was a lot of shouting and ordering them to open up, but they wouldn't do anything till I came back. That's when they threatened to kill David and the rest of our group. Some had started to throw stones at the castle, but none hit our people.

Nathan saw us arrive and told Tom we were in trouble. That's when Steve fired the shot to lure the roamers to the attackers. Nathan continued to watch out for us. He saw the hoard coming for the castle en-masse. That's when all hell broke loose.

"What happened to David and their leader?"

"He ran off like a coward, while his people fought for their lives. He let David go, but I've not seen him, he could be part of that lot," he pointed over his shoulder towards the gate.

I wondered: was it him I met in the farm? That meant he could return.

I then asked about Nathan, Rachael and Emily.

"They're good people," Tom said. "Nathan worked hard while you were gone, and he's the one who put them in that corner. Rachael is a kind soul; she's always ready to get her hands dirty. Emily is quiet, but she works well. Neave seems to like her, she always wants to play, and Emily seems to enjoy it. You can trust them," he said, matter of fact.

"Okay, Tom, I trust you, so I'll trust them." I walked away towards the group of prisoners.

There were three men and a woman; they all had a look of hate about them. It worried me.

I pointed to the largest man and told him to stand. He was

a good ten centimetres taller than me, walking up to him. I stayed an arm's length away and asked who they were.

"Fuck off," he said and smiled.

I stepped a little closer. "Who are you, and why did you come here?"

"Fuck off."

A step closer, "Who are you," not a question this time, just a statement.

"Fuck o ..."

I punched him in the stomach, he doubled over. I pointed to the next size down, "Who are you?"

"Go fuck yourself," he said, with equal bravado.

I turned and walked away, "Kill them," I said flatly.

Kelly re-cocked her rifle, a round flew out and another slid into the chamber.

"Okay, I'll tell you," said the large man.

I walked back; I'm so glad Kelly never questioned my command. "Well?"

"We're just a group trying to survive, like you," he said. "Your man walked into our camp, telling us how safe the castle was, and that you had plenty of food and medical supplies. Duncan wanted to take it over for us."

"Where was your camp?"

"In one of the houses at the back there," he pointed over the back of the castle. "It's in the grounds of a big house. Duncan lives there, I think. Some of us live in the house, the others camp in the grounds."

"How did you get food?"

"From the other houses, there are quite a few of them with massive pantries."

"What about the dead, how did you deal with them?"

"We would go out in force and kill as many as we could see."

"This Duncan, who is he?"

"Not really sure, he picked us up one day. Said if we worked for him, we'd be safe."

"Have you attacked other people before?"

He was quiet for a while. The other people with him seemed to be trying to communicate by thought alone.

"Yes, a group in Glenfield. They killed our people, who then turned and killed us even more." He must have seen my face change: "That was you?" he said, aghast. "Only a couple of people got out alive. They said there were more of you, about twenty."

The others dropped their heads.

"No, this is us. We were just ready for you, and made our escape. I should kill you here and now."

I turned and walked away. I went to the gate and saw David's remains crawling towards me, snapping its teeth. I drew my pistol and shot him in the head. He was now with Marie.

The roamers were still outside in large numbers, and the shot made them agitated. *How were we going to get out?* I didn't want to shoot every one of them and waste bullets.

I went back to the prisoners and stood looking at them a while, thinking. I told Jess and Kelly to guard them a little longer. Then I'd get them swapped out. Josie gave me a cup of tea, I thanked her.

"You're still wet, go and change," she told me, so off I went to my tent.

Rachael was there with Neave. "Granddad," she shouted and ran, jumping into my arms. "Eh, granddad all wet," but she still gave me a big hug.

I loved this little girl; she always made me smile. I hugged her back.

"Gramps needs to change; go back to granny," I said.

"It's Nanna," said Rachael. "Granny makes me sound old," we laughed, and I went to change.

I'd made up my mind: I did not want to kill unarmed people, but what should we do? Using cable ties, we secured our prisoners and made them comfortable. I needed to show that we weren't like them. We even gave them food and water.

We all sat around the fire, eating dinner and keeping warm – the nights were getting colder. I wanted to check out the two farms that we passed earlier in the afternoon, but things had changed.

"We need to get rid of the roamers outside. And what do we do with our new friends?" I nodded in the direction of the prisoners.

"Shoot them," said Josie, which shocked me as much as it did the others.

"Don't want to waste ammo on the roamers, there's too many of them," said Paul.

"No, not them, *them*," she said, pointing to the prisoners.

"We're not killing unarmed people," I interjected.

"Give them something then," she continued.

"Josie," said Flo, "where is this coming from, this is not like you?"

"It's bastards like them that killed my Frank!"

There was a hush over the camp. Josie had never talked about her life before, and this was a first.

"No, I'm letting them go in the morning."

"What if they come back," said my Rachael.

"We'll be long gone by then, and this place won't be worth anything when we do." I looked around the group. "But we need to get by the dead outside first, any ideas?"

Nathan put his hand up. It made me smile. "You're not at school, Nathan," I stated, jokingly. He put his hand down and started going red.

"Distraction," he said. "If someone could make a lot of noise somewhere in the village, it may ... no, it *will* draw them away."

"Brilliant idea, we'll go with that," I said; Nathan smiled.

So the plan was drawn up, Nathan, Rachael Two and Tony were going to swim across the moat to the farm. Tony would be the only one to have a gun – he was the only trained person. If they met anyone, dead or alive, they were to shoot on sight and make as much noise as possible. They were then to find the car that we left and drive it around, sounding the horn, drawing the dead away. This was my way of making sure Nathan and Rachael were part of the team. I trusted what the others said, but I needed to be sure.

People were starting to get tired, but I wanted to talk about London. I wanted to find out about the virus and see if there was a cure. This started a long discussion about the pros and cons. Some liked the idea of a road trip, as they were starting to get tired of the same four walls. It was a metaphor for life.

It was the oldies that wanted to go the most, which surprised me. The younger ones wanted to stay, Jess being one of them. However, she did say she would go, as she felt safer with me and the group. The others agreed with her, if it came down to a choice. As a group we were stronger, but we all needed to be strong before we went. Paul needed to heal, and others needed training, so we made another plan.

Once we'd gotten rid of the dead outside, we would travel to the farm we'd seen on the way to Markfield. We'd go a roundabout route to make sure that we were not followed. Then we'd stay there through the winter. In the spring, the weather would be warm enough to sleep outside and we could move on.

Chapter Thirteen

The distraction team swam the moat once the sun was high. We watched them run to the car, and I saw Tony shoot a couple of roamers on the way. The ones near the gate turned to the sound of the noise, but only a couple started to move off.

Once at the car, Rachael Two got in the driver's seat. With the windows rolled down, they started to shout and sound the horn as they drove along. More of the dead moved towards them, as Rachael drove down the road leading to the castle, she turned the car and waited. The noise was brilliant. Tony shot a few more dead just to help with the distraction.

Nathan got out of the car and ran around like a madman. When they saw food, the roamers quickened their pace. He kept just ahead of them until he got back to the car, then he jumped in. It moved off slowly; they even let the dead touch the boot. Tony was leaning out shooting at them, while Nathan was shouting out the other side.

It worked: the roamers were following the car. Once on the main street, they would weave down one of the side roads, and leave the throng there. Once that was done, they would meet us at the junction on the far side of the village. Then we'd make our way to the farm, going the way we came back from the quarry.

As soon as the monsters were out of sight, we quickly moved the loaded cars. We had taken down the tents and loaded them up first thing. Opening the gates, we backed up the lorry and then the APC, loading them up one at a time. It took a lot longer than I liked: it was nearly an hour. I just hoped the group outside were okay. I'd not heard any noise for a good twenty minutes.

Everyone climbed into a vehicle. I let Tom drive the lorry, as he had driven large vehicles in the past. The lorry and APC were very loud – again I hoped that it wouldn't draw the dead back. We raced as fast as the slowest vehicle would go, which was the APC. It was in the lead; Jess was on the .50 cal. Kelly was manning the machine gun on the lorry, which was bringing up the tail. Steve was in the back as rear guard.

Halfway down Main Street, the dead started to wander out of the side streets. We would leave them alone unless they got too close. We came to the junction: left took you to Leicester Forest East, and right took you to Desford. We were going right – there sat the car, waiting, with Tony standing guard. As soon as we came into sight, he waved and jumped into the car. As we passed, they joined the ranks. I was so glad they had made it. My main worry was that Duncan and his group would have heard them and laid an ambush. They were safe now; we could all get to the farm.

Back at the castle, I left the prisoners with a knife and a pistol with one full clip. They should've been able to cut themselves free and get back to Duncan safely – if they didn't attract too much attention from the dead. Yes, I had left them as bait, but only to draw the dead back, not to be eaten. It was the best thing I could have done. They may have followed or tried to stop us. I couldn't leave it to chance. If the tables were turned, they would have killed all of us with no mercy. At least, for the time being, they were alive.

With me in the front driving the APC, Paul followed in one car. Then came the distraction team, with my Rachael driving the last car. Tom with Flo took up the rear in the lorry; we were quite a convoy. If we were followed, Steve was to fire a magazine until it emptied. Tom was then to flash his lights, and so on down the chain. People were only to stop when the lead vehicle stopped. We would then face our followers.

Having travelled past the Desford Tubes, a factory that closed down years ago but still remained, we turned right. We wound our way through the villages, but instead of going through Thornton, we turned right and passed the reservoir. I didn't want to go through Markfield and meet the hoard again. The last thing I wanted was them following us and finally getting to the farms. We arrived at the houses we'd seen yesterday and turned right, down the road. Again, we had a safe journey, only seeing the odd roamer.

On arrival at the first farm, I saw that the house had solid walls around it, and they were in good repair – *nice*. I turned the APC so it faced the road. The others did the same. Jess and Kelly stayed on their guns. Steve went to the gate and watched the road both ways. I told everyone to stay in the cars until Tony, Jayne and I returned. We had to make sure that the house was clear, before we unloaded and made it in to our home for the winter.

I went first and checked the two barns, clear. I closed the doors. Now, on to the house: it sat at the back of the court-yard. To the right was a stable block – *great, somewhere for the stores*. The yard was closed with sturdy iron gates; they squealed as I opened them. I waved Tony and Jayne in.

A roamer, it was a woman, came out of a door to the right side of the house. Jayne took it out with one shot. The sound drew out three more, two men and a boy. I stopped them shooting and drew out my machete. They took out knives. I did the boy, Jayne and Tony the others. I felt a little sick: I had never killed a child before. I reminded myself that this was not the boy who had lived: this was a monster that would have killed any of us.

We waited a little while then moved on to the stables; there were five in all. Each stable had a half eaten horse in it. Then we moved into the house. The door the woman roamer came out of was the kitchen. Through that, we moved into the dining room, then living room. There were five bedrooms; all were clear.

We went back out to the group and told them to start unloading. I told them not to go into the stables just yet because of the horses. I did ask them to remove the bodies of the dead first. The girls were to stay on guard, as was Steve.

We went around the back of the house, and what a sight for sore eyes: two massive gas tanks. Both of them were full when we checked. Cooked food and heat, it was going to be hard to leave in the spring. The rest of the farm was clear. The neighbouring place looked similar to this one. I looked over the hedge and saw it was quiet for the moment; we'd check it tomorrow.

All the vehicles unloaded, we moved the dead horses, cleaned out the stables and put the stores into them. Mary had started on making dinner and had hot tea and coffee waiting. We turned the dining room into a bedroom; we would have to share until we cleared the other house. We made a rota for guard duty. At the moment, it was on the APC, but I removed the .50 cal, and people would use their personal weapons.

Jayne was on guard first. When she shouted for us to come out, we all came running, with weapons drawn, thinking: *not trouble already*. She was pointing to the roof of the house. We turned, looked up and saw solar panels – we would have electric as well. We'd fallen lucky with this place.

We went in and started to switch lights on, giggling like school children. Six months without electricity and look how happy we were! *How sad were we?* After dinner, we changed the guard and settled down to listen to some music on a CD player. This was the life.

The next morning, we cleared the other farmhouse. It too had gas but not solar panels. We found six roamers: two women, the rest were men. In the two barns, we found half-eaten cows and a tractor with a trailer. I wanted to remove the bodies and take them far away to burn. The smoke would be seen for miles.

After lunch, my Rachael, Paul and I went off to see how much land there was and how far it went. We crossed the field to the hedge line, and we saw the M1 motorway on the other side. We made our way to the right and came across a track with a bridge over the motorway. We followed that for about half a mile, and there, in the middle of a small wood, was a caravan park. There were a few roamers, so we killed them – the strange thing was that they were all naked. There was a house to the left, so we checked it out, and it was clear. We found nothing else useful for the time being.

There was a footpath going through the back, so we followed the yellow signs until we came upon a small pond. As we stood there, carp were surfacing. Paul said that he was going to find a fishing rod and catch some of them to eat. It would be good to have fresh food.

To the left of us was a smallholding; we went and had a look. Three roamers this time, and we dealt with them quickly. Paul found his fishing rod plus plenty of gear. He put them near the pond for now and would come back later to fish – he was one happy bunny.

There seemed to be a small community out here, so we had to clear all the houses and outbuildings. It made me wonder how the virus got here, to all these places in the back of beyond. They should have been safe, but all it took was one bite or someone dying. More questions were forming about the virus: was it airborne? London was on the cards now, for sure.

As we crossed more fields, I saw Ratby to our left. Rachael said she knew where we were, it was a place called the Burrows. She pointed to her right and said that a golf course was over that way. She was pretty sure that Kirby was in front of us. I was interested in the golf course: it could be a place to burn the bodies of the dead, and the horses and cows.

We headed towards the golf course, when we saw yet another small farm. From where we stood, we could see living horses and cows. Paul said that we had to check it out. If no one was there, we'd have beef as well, more than enough to last the winter. So off we went.

There was a large, metal gate, which was open, so we walked straight through. We drew our weapons just in case we got attacked. There was nobody around; the place was empty.

It was more a farm *mansion* than house. It had full gas tanks and solar panels. From an attic room you could see for miles – the guard wouldn't get cold. We had a quick chat about moving; there were no dead bodies to burn, we could just leave them at the other place. It was clean – well, a little dusty perhaps – and we all would have a room each. We made the decision to live here for the winter.

We walked back down the road that led to the house. It ran for about two miles, bringing us to Ratby. At the bottom were a pub and a school. I didn't fancy walking through the village, so we turned back and headed the way we came, back through the caravan park.

By the time we got back, it was starting to get dark, and I could see lights on in the house. Nathan was on guard; he had my sword. I called him in so we could all talk about our day and what we had found.

Chapter Fourteen

We moved to the new farmhouse the next day. Everyone was happy with what we had found. We were thankful not to be moving the horses and cows – they had gone rotten. Over the winter, it was very quiet for us. The odd roamer would turn up. We simply shut the gate, and they never bothered us. The house was a good 300 metres from the gate and fence, so we kept movement to a minimum.

Paul went fishing, bringing carp home, and we slaughtered a cow. The house had freezers, so once it was butchered we could save the meat. We also tried to keep the lights to a minimum, as it would attract others if they saw them at night. I felt assured though: not many people would be walking around in the middle of nowhere, at night, in the winter.

We talked about life before the virus, laughing and crying at peoples' stories. We found out that Josie's husband was murdered by a gang of thugs back in the Eighties. They had been terrorising the neighbourhood; he went out and told them to leave. By the time the police got there, they had kicked him to death, cutting off his ears as trophies. She pleaded with them to stop, but they just laughed at her, telling her that she was next. That was when the police arrived – they had quite a battle on their hands. Over a hundred police were eventually drafted in to deal with the gang. Some escaped, but most were arrested. But it never brought Frank back.

Tom, as we knew, had been a policeman, a very good one

at that. Solving crimes, he became a detective at 25 with the vice squad. He didn't like it there, as he had to deal with child porn and slavery. He started to have bad dreams and became depressed. He was moved over to another unit and became a brilliant murder detective. He seemed to have the ability to understand the way that killers thought. He would only see bodies once, so it didn't affect him as much, even in child killings. Flo was a good, old housewife. She looked after Tom, and as they had no children, they lived a comfortable life.

Paul was a landscape gardener. He had his own business that he inherited from his father, who started it in the '70s. Marie was his business partner; she took calls and did all the accounts. He was one of the dearest out there, but you got what you paid for. Paul only used the best materials and always inspected the job himself. He made his men do it again if it wasn't right, at no extra cost to the customer. His men learned early to get the job right and never to cut corners. He would sack people on the spot for doing just that. He never needed to advertise, as word of mouth got him a lot of business. He never had a slump in trade; he was always working.

Kelly and Steve were a hard-working couple: she a teaching assistant and he a shop fitter. He travelled the country, working, so he spent a lot of time away. When the outbreak started, he quickly came home to be with Kelly.

Tony and Jayne: another hard working couple. They had two children that were killed in a car accident two-years ago. They were only just coming to terms with it. Tony was a semi-self-taught carpenter; his father was a cabinet maker and taught him how to work with wood. Over the years, Tony became an odd-job man, and because he was so good, people always wanted him for work. He could mend just about anything – he was even a good mechanic. Jayne was a cleaning manager with a national company. She was contracted over schools and other council-run buildings.

Nathan and Rachael were newlyweds. She was a bar manager at a night club, and he was still at university, studying to be a lawyer. Emily was Rachael's cousin; she worked at a day nursery. That's why she was so good with Neave.

I told the group who I was and some of my stories of covert operations and bodyguard duties of the rich and famous, royals, and politicians. They asked a lot of questions, which I answered, some of them bound by the official secrets act, but that was not something to worry about now. They also asked if I'd killed people. I told them that I had but only in battle, or to stop them hurting others. And yes, I had done an assassination, a crime lord in South America who ran guns, drugs and people.

We also talked about the trip to London: which route to take; what to do if we found survivors on the way, whether they were friendly or not; how would we decide where to stop and camp; what would we take with us; how would we travel; what might we find.

We knew there would be a lot of dead people roaming around, but we didn't know about the government. Would they be in bunkers underground, or would they be all dead? When were we going to leave? Over the winter months, these questions developed into answers.

To travel, we would take the APC and lorry. We would also try to find a minibus – the fewer vehicles the better. On the lorry, we would carry supplies, tents and fuel. The APC would carry all of the ammunition and spare weapons; and the minibus, the people. We would travel down the motorway and use the service stations to rest up. As a rule, it only took you two hours to travel to London from Leicester. That was travelling at 70 miles an hour, but we didn't know how bad any abandoned cars would be. Travelling would be slow going no matter what – the APC's maximum speed was 50, but I wasn't going to push it.

If the motorway was too bad we would have to find alternative routes. If we found survivors, we would cross that bridge when we got to it. Some might want to come with us, others may not. If they were aggressive, we would take them out before they hurt us. We had the firepower. Everyone was taught to use all of the weapons we had collected, even the sniper rifles. Nathan turned out to be a cracking shot. We all decided to leave when the weather became warmer – either April or May.

Chapter Fifteen

The winter remained uneventful. It snowed over December and January, so we stayed in the farmhouse – we did not want to leave tracks for people to follow. When the snow melted at last, we started to prepare for the road trip. We used the cars to do supply runs, slowly building up our medicine and food stocks. We also found new tents and bedding for the trip, and siphoned as much fuel as we could.

Mid-March, I got a call from the attic lookout: it was Rachael Two. When I arrived, she was pointing towards the gates. There was a man looking through the railings. I grabbed the binoculars from the shelf and peered through: his face was a little fuzzy with the distance, but I could tell he was young. I called down through the hatch for everyone to stop and remain still for a bit. The downstairs went quiet.

"How long has he been there?" I asked Rachael.

"About two minutes, he walked from the left, there ..." she pointed towards the entrance road. "Then he looked around himself and stopped at the gates. That's when I called you."

Still looking through the glasses, I could see he was shouting. Then I heard him. He was calling, "Hello, is anyone there?" but he got no reply. He stopped shouting and rattled the gates; they were heavy and well padlocked. He just stood there looking up at us. *Did he know we were there, and why was he on his own?*

On second glance at him, I noticed that he had no weapons,

no supplies, and he looked reasonably clean. *Where were the others? Was this one of Duncan's group? Had a search party sent him in to investigate the area*? If we took him in they would know; if we killed him they would know. If we just let him go would they know we were there?

I told Rachael to watch him while I went to other parts of the house. Luckily, there were net curtains at the windows, so we could see out and no one could see in. I went to each side of the house and scanned the area to see if anyone was hiding. As I passed people, I told them what was happening and told them to watch for movement. We could see nothing.

He stayed for twenty minutes, shouting and rattling the gates. He looked back up the road he had come from and moved off. If he was just travelling through and stumbled on our house, he would have carried on the way he was going, but he went back the way he came. This told me he had an agenda. We waited another twenty minutes then Paul, Nathan, Tony and I left through the back of the house, through a rear entrance we had made for quick escapes.

We circled the area and made our way to the drive. I knew we'd miss them, but I was hoping to find signs. They had a vehicle, and it had stopped in a small car park; I could see where they had flattened the weeds. We had to be careful – there was open ground between us and the main road. If we stayed close to the hedgerow, we may not be seen.

At the bottom of the hill was a small ford, then the road went up again. We took our time getting to the top. Once there, we crawled to the brow and looked down to the main road. At the bottom were the pub and school.

From where we were, we could see three cars with people standing around them. We each had binoculars and were looking through them. I could make out the boy who was at the gate and I could also make out Duncan. The boy was pointing our way and so was Duncan. They seemed to be talking about what was up here.

After what seemed a lifetime, they climbed into the cars and drove off. *Phew, that was close. But what did they know?* I wondered if they had seen us coming and going. I doubted it, as we went the back way most of the time. They could have possibly seen us when we brought the bigger stuff back.

"They could have been in hiding, just waiting to see if we came and went," said Tom.

We were having a meeting about the incident and its ramifications.

"Yes, but how did they know?" said Paul.

"What if they just saw us by chance?" Jayne pondered. "I know we are careful when we come back, but what if they came round the corner just as the last vehicle drove up?"

We all agreed on this point, as it was the only way they might have known.

What to do now?

"It's too early to leave; we're not ready yet," said my Rachael. There were nods all around.

There was a pause as people thought about the situation. I knew what I wanted to do, but that was my old army training. I just wanted to see what the others would come up with.

Jess looked at me for help, then a light went on in her head. "Dad, in that old television show about the SAS, the one with Ross Kemp ..."

I smiled, yes I remembered that, quite close to the truth but over the top. I narrowed my eyes at her and said, "Yes?"

"Well, I remember one where they made a hideout in the bushes, could we do that?"

"You mean an OP?" an observation post. "We could, but

we would need a means of communication and time to make it. Its open ground around there and it's only the hedge for cover," I said. This is what I wanted: I needed the group to start thinking for themselves. If something happened to me, they had to be able to survive.

Nathan spoke, "I know where there are some radios. At the golf course! I saw them in the office when we last went there for shooting practice!" He was beaming.

"Great," I said, "you go and get them in the morning with Rach Two, Emily and Paul." I could see him raise himself with pride. "Be careful, and don't get caught. Go the back way, and circle round to it. Tony, Jess, Jayne and I will check out a good site for the OP. When you lot come back with the radios, we'll make one."

Early morning, the four went off to the golf course and we went to scout out an OP. Before we moved out, I checked with Tom, who was on watch in the attic. I asked if there had been any movement. He said there hadn't. We went out the back way to be on the safe side.

We crossed into the meadow and walked the edge. When we came to the car park we went onto the road. We sat and waited ten minutes and then made our way to the brow of the hill. Again, we watched through binoculars and waited another ten minutes. I told Jayne to keep an eye on the entrance to the road.

There was a drainage ditch on the left side of the road, it was just under a metre deep and full of weeds, grass and water. On the other side was another hedge, it was quite thick. We walked back a bit to an opening and looked at the other side. On this side was a ditch, the same as the one before. We could cut some of the hedge out and make an OP in there. By putting the cuttings in the ditch, it would make a dry crossing.

I heard my name called, so we went back to Jayne. Crawling next to her, we had a view down the road to the pub. A small group of roamers had started to walk up the hill; looking through my binoculars I counted six. I signalled to Tony and Jess to stay where they were and be quiet.

As we watched them walk up the hill, one wandered over to the ditch and fell in. It went head first, all I could see were its legs kicking the air. The others just carried on. I drew my knife out, and Jayne followed suit. I motioned Jayne into the ditch and I slid in after her. I whispered that I didn't want to kill them unless we had to. I didn't want to leave signs of our presence. I was starting to feel cold, with the water up to my chest, and I started to shiver. I could see Jayne was just as bad. I put my arms around her and tried to share body heat, it helped a little.

We watched the roamers wander by; one of them lifted its head as if to smell the air. It moved over to the hedge where the other two were, starting to reach out through the foliage, groaning and moaning. The others turned as if they'd been told food was through there. All five were clawing at the bushes, hissing. I saw a hand plunge its knife into the head of one, then another did the same. Jayne and I jumped out of the ditch, ran over to the hedge and killed the other three.

Tony and Jess came round to our side and looked down at the bodies.

"Not done that for a while," said Tony, tapping one of the bodies with his foot to make sure it was dead.

"We'll have to move the bodies," I said. We grabbed a couple and put them into the ditch farther down the hill, hoping they rotted away out of sight.

I put Tony and Jess on guard while Jayne and I went back to the house to dry off and get fresh clothes. Then we would come back with Steve and Kelly to help build the OP. I told

Tony and Jess that if they saw anyone turn up, to get back to the house ASAP. On the walk back, we saw movement in the bushes on the road leading to the golf course. We stopped and drew our guns, out popped Paul with Nathan, Emily and Rachael in tow.

"Hi buddy," said Paul, "gave us a scare then, thought you were the enemy."

"No, just us drowned rats, are they the radios?" I asked, pointing at the bag Nathan was carrying.

"Yes, but they need charging. Just hope they work once we've done it; they may have been left too long.

We took them back to the house with us. I gave Nathan the job of sorting out the radios as he seemed to have some knowledge about them. I told Steve and Kelly to sort out the tools and equipment for the OP, then go meet up with Jess and Tony. They were to all wait for me. I then put Rachael Two and Jayne on attic duty to give Tom a rest.

My Rachael was playing with Neave in the play room and Emily went in to them. Neave seemed to like Emily and Emily her; Neave had started to call her 'aunty'. We made her her own playroom, so she wasn't around adults all the time. The rest were doing housework, getting food ready and doing the laundry. I felt a little sexist that the women were doing the mundane stuff, but they seemed happy with it and took it over from the start.

It only took us a couple of hours to complete the OP. From the field side of the hedge, if you knew what to look for, you would see it, but at a glance you wouldn't know. From the road side you couldn't see a thing. We brought down the rest of the group to check it out. We didn't tell them where it was and they all walked by it on both sides – we were happy.

I took first watch in the OP and Steve was to relieve me

at midnight. The next day, the radios were fully charged and worked a treat. Nathan took over as control, manning the base station in the house. Steve and Tony went out and tested the range. They went over two miles and still came in clear. The next time went on a supply run, we'd see how much farther they would go, but for now they were great.

Over the next week, we saw no sign of Duncan's group. Were they still checking other places, or were they just biding their time, watching the entrance to the road? As we were unsure, we used the back way out more often and never used the road. If we had large stuff we would use the tractor. It was noisy, but it saved our backs.

Chapter Sixteen

The back end of March is when we saw a little action. Tom called through on the radio; he and Jess were on OP duty. They had seen two cars coming up the road. I called up to the attic and asked them if they saw anything. Nothing yet, came a reply from Rachael One.

Everyone got into the positions we had been practising – everyone had a window to defend, so we had all-round protection. Rachael called, vehicles were coming in now. I went to a front window, Josie was at this one and I could see the cars clearly. One was a red Mondeo, the other a white Audi. Three people got out of each car, all young men, from about eighteen to mid-twenties. Two were carrying guns; I tried to get a good look. One was a shotgun, the other an air rifle. Depending on the make, the air rifle could be as lethal as a gun at close range. Over a distance, it was not very good; the same with the shotgun.

They stood looking at the house. One pointed to my right; had they seen a curtain twitch? They shook the gate and started to shout.

A tall man with short hair was doing the shouting, "We know someone is in there, we can see movement at the window." He pointed to my right.

Who was there? I thought for a second, it was Paul.

"We only want to be part of your group. We've been camping all winter and just want to feel safe," he shouted.

I went to other windows, Paul's first, and told him to be still.

"Sorry, mate, I slipped and nearly fell out the window," he gave a sheepish smile.

I then went downstairs and looked out. Nathan was next to me, lying on the table with the sniper rifle; his eye never left the sight. "I could take them all out from here," he said.

I went to the front door and looked through the glass. I took off my holster and put my pistol in the back of my trousers, it felt snug at the small of my back. I put the radio on a shelf next to the door. Opening the front door, I put up my hands and went out.

I walked slowly up to the gates. I didn't smile or look menacing; I just tried to look neutral. I gave each person the quick once over. No way had they been camping, they looked too clean, a little shabby but clean.

One of the faces shocked me.

The group turned to the young man, his face was as shocked as mine. I knew him. I thought he was dead, but he wasn't, he stood in front of me.

The man who had been shouting said, "Do you know this freak?"

"Yes," he replied, "he's my father-in-law."

I brought myself round, "Hello Jason, wish you'd come with us now, do you?"

He smiled a little, he knew I wasn't keen on him, but I was always courteous for Jess' sake. She saw something in him which I couldn't, so I let it go.

The man in charge pulled him forward, "Tell him we need his help, we're hungry and near death."

They looked well fed to me.

Jason walked up to the gate, "How's Jess and the baby? Are they still alive?" he mumbled. He always mumbled, half the time I had to ask him to repeat himself.

"They're doing well. Jess has killed plenty of roamers – she's quite the warrior now. And Neave is a great kid, none of this crap has fazed her."

"That's great," he mumbled, "can we come in please, we really need help?"

He looked me in the eyes, I could see he was trying to say something, he had never looked me in the eyes before. I had to think fast: I didn't want him killed by them or me, so I had to do something quick. I stood in front of him and scratched my head. I held three fingers up. Five seconds later, three lay dead on the floor, the two with guns and the main man. That left three standing.

I pulled out my gun as the men looked down at the dead bodies. They went to go for the guns and I shot a round in front of them. They stopped.

"You two go back to Duncan and tell him if he wants this place he's got a war to fight. Every window has a gun pointed at you; we have massive firepower. You have an air rifle and a shot gun. I'll keep Jason here as a hostage. I'll only talk to your leader, now go, or you'll be next."

They ran to the Mondeo and drove off at speed. Once out of sight, I opened the gate and took Jason in.

"Don't say a word, or I will kill you, OK? Just march up to the house and keep your hands on your head." I relocked the gates, "Go."

We walked back to the house; I kept my pistol trained on him. Once back in, I radioed Jess to get back from the OP and then told Steve and Kelly to change with Tom.

I took Jason to the dining room and was cable-tying his hands to the chair when Jess came in.

"I heard gunshots ... and that car left fast. I saw the bodies at the ..." she never finished the sentence, shocked at who she saw in the chair.

Walking around to face him, she looked into his eyes; she was cold and hard. She slapped his face and walked out, then I heard her start to cry. I radioed up for Rachael to go to Jess, then told Tony to cover the attic.

I stood in front of him, he looked small and sorry for himself. His eyes never left my feet.

"First of all, how did you survive after the outbreak? Then I want to know everything about this Duncan: what has he planned for us and how many people does he control?"

He shrugged his shoulders, "Just got out and met a group of people. We roamed around for a bit and then found this group." He was never much of a talker. He thought he was right, even when he knew he wasn't, and he would do the opposite of what anyone told him. This lad made my teeth grind.

"Stop talking shit," I was in his face, less than a centimetre away from his nose. "I want the whole story, or you're back with that gang out there. I'll bet top dollar they won't be happy that you know me, hey?"

He shrunk into himself; I saw a tear forming at the edge of his left eye. He was scared – of me, yes, but more so of them. He knew I wouldn't kill him, but they would.

"After you took Jess and Neave, I sat watching the telly. There was nothing on but the outbreak, every channel was the same. I started to wish I'd gone with you, but was too scared to call, so I just waited. The phone rang a few times, but I never answered. Three days later, the army started to knock on doors, telling us to either get out of the city or make sure our doors were locked. I made a run for it; I was going to go to yours, but was soon caught up with a group of people from the street. There were about twelve of us, we started to walk to the suburbs. Quite a few got kill by the dead. I nearly got caught out but ran for it. We made our way to Glenfield, as I knew you might be there with Jess, but we kept getting into trouble with other people and geeks. We broke into houses to find food and shelter. It took nearly a week to get to Glenfield, and by then only four of us were left."

He was really opening up. I listened without saying a word.

"We bumped into a group that wanted to help us; they had cars and lots of supplies, so we stayed with them. They told us of a settlement of people who had set up a street, and they were going to try and take it. But we were too small, so the main man wanted to recruit more people. He was camped up at school grounds in Groby. By the time I got there, there must have been about twenty people, both men and women. Some of them were tough, real-criminal types; some of them were killers. I saw people being beaten – they even had a hanging tree, three bodies were hanging from it. They had turned into geeks, people would go up to them, stabbing and cutting parts off. That's when I found out you have to kill the brain to stop them from moving.

Jason paused, recalling his experience and the horrid details. I just let him continue.

"After a few weeks, our numbers had grown. That's when Duncan wanted to attack the street in Glenfield. The talk was that survivors were seen coming from the hospital. That's how they were found. So he sent a load of his people to go and take it over, but they weren't ready for the reception they got. Only a few escaped. Their leader killed a couple before the main attack and they turned into geeks, attacking our own people. The survivors we were after made a run for it and escaped very quickly, but they did leave loads of stuff behind. We cleaned up the street of the geeks, took what we needed and burned the street down so that they could never come back."

I sat impassively while I listened to his recount of our street's downfall, wondering if he'd figured it out.

"We then found a posh housing estate and moved in there. It was a lot more comfortable than the school. We took over a few properties and settled in. One day we saw smoke coming from the back of us, so Duncan sent a scouting party to see what it was. When they came back, they said that there was a group at the castle. They also said that there was an armoured car there, as well as a big lorry. Then this bloke turned up saying he was from the castle. He hoped we could team up. He said that some of his group had gone to find guns. Duncan liked the idea of guns, so we all went to attack the place, but a load of geeks attacked us. I only just got away."

Again, Jason paused, I wanted him to continue, so I said, "Go on."

"We went back a couple of days later, after two of our group returned with a gun and told us the castle people had done a runner. They only just made it out: one of them got caught by geeks. They told us how the castle lot distracted the geeks away from them. We used the same plan, but when we got there, there was nothing to have – everything had been taken. We took back our minibuses and went home. Over the next few weeks, we were sent out to look for the castle group."

Inhaling then breathing out long and slow, he went on, "It was before the snow: we saw people come up here – there was even smoke coming from the chimney. The snow fell, so we left it alone until now; we had our own problems over winter. We kept a guard at the bottom of the road, to see if people came and went. And we did. So when the weather turned, Duncan and some others drove up to the place to check it out. They saw movement and even saw a cow being slaughtered. That's when he wanted the place for himself. He wanted fresh food, to cook on gas and have electric. We couldn't have all stayed here, but he wanted it for himself. When he sent James up to see if anyone would come out and they didn't, he was furious. He had him hanged because he couldn't tell him anything. That's why we came here today. The two you sent back will be dead by now. That's why I'm glad you kept me. He rules with an iron fist. If you don't do what he says, he kills you. People have tried to leave. He lets them go, then sends his death squad after them. I just kept my head down and never went against him, till now. If I go back, I'll be a geek and they'll cut me to bits." There were tears running down his face.

I asked if he'd killed any people and he shook his head. I asked about the roamers and he had, loads of times to save his or someone else's life.

"What about weapons? I already know about the ones from earlier, do they have other guns, and if they do, what type?"

"They have a load of air rifles they found in peoples' homes and some air pistols too. They've got a few shotguns – they were found in farms and some houses."

"So, how many do they have?"

He thought for a while, looking up at the ceiling and then he said, "I would say about twelve shotguns and about ten air rifles and pistols."

"What about ammunition?"

"Not much, really, a couple of boxes for the shotguns, and a few tins of pellets for the others. They wasted a lot, when they first got them, on the geeks. Then Duncan started to control the use of them. Only the main people have them; everyone else has to use knives or metal stakes."

"How many people does he control now?"

"There are about 150 of us ... well, *them*. His main people are the criminals. There's about twelve of them. They're the ones who do the punishing and stuff. They get all the girls and all the good gear and food. Each man has a small group he runs. The man out there was my boss. He's killed loads – really mean he was."

I nodded and changed the questioning. "Does this *Duncan* have use of any other things that could cause us trouble, big lorries or anything like that?"

"He does have a bin lorry we use to ram open gates and doors. It's one of the ones that lifts the bins over its back with two huge things at the front."

I knew the type. "Anything else you can think of?"

Again, he thought. I could see he was racking his brain, but then he shook his head, "No, that's it."

"Right, if you do think of anything, big or small, I want to know. For now, you stay in here. I'll take off the cuffs, but you don't go anywhere without someone with you, OK?"

He nodded. I undid the cable ties and left the room.

I called everyone together for a meeting, except for the people in the OP. I told them what Jason had said. We needed to draw up a defence plan, because I knew this Duncan would try to come and in force this time. He would bring everyone he had. We had great firepower, but sometimes sheer numbers can overwhelm a position.

Chapter Seventeen

The weather started to warm up by April, so we made the decision to leave before Duncan and his hoards decided to attack. We all agreed to fight if it came to it; we knew he would kill us all. Tony serviced the APC and lorry, along with the cars. We couldn't find any minibuses in the time we had left. We placed the APC at the front of the house, on the drive. If they came with the bin wagon, the .50 cal would kill the engine and do some damage before it reached us.

Nathan made sure all the radios were fully charged, so we could use them on the way down to London. Jason was kept under guard by Steve, Paul, Tony or me. We made him do his own chores to keep him busy, but there was very little trust of him. Even from Jess, she hardly spoke to him and wouldn't let Neave see him.

People came and went, all checking the place out. Sometimes three or more, but they never came too close. We left the bodies of their dead at the gates as a warning. Paul and Steve would go around in the woods, checking for intruders, but they only ever seemed to use the main road in.

We had never been so on edge – we wondered when they were going to come. Sometimes we'd talk, saying that we'd wish they would just do it and get it over with. At the same time, we started to pack and load the lorry and cars, ready for the push. As soon as we were ready, we'd be gone.

Everything was ready for the go. The OP reported the

normal two cars at the bottom of the road. I called them back to the house, Tom and Nathan; they were with us in minutes. Tom said that there were no changes at the road. Everyone got into their vehicles.

In the front was the APC, with me driving and my Rachael on the .50 cal. Next, in the first car, were Paul, Rose, Josie and Mary. In the next car were Tom and Flo, with Jess, Neave and Emily. The last car was driven by Tony and Jayne, with Jason cable tied and made to lie down on the back seat. Last came the lorry: Steve would be driving, with Kelly on the machine gun. In the back, giving rear support, were Nathan and Rachael Two.

Rachael Two opened the gates and the engines started up. She ran to the lorry and climbed in the back with Nathan. We were going to go straight to the motorway: back through Kirby Muxloe, on to the A46 ring road, and then south to London.

I called to Rachael: as soon as she saw the cars at the bottom, she was to start firing. Hopefully, people would scatter when the heavy-calibre bullets started whizzing around their ears. As we came over the crest of the hill, facing downwards, I saw the cars, one either side of the road. There must have been about six people moving. They'd heard the engines coming, but now they saw us they seemed to be panicking.

Rachael started to let loose the big gun. She just took her time: pop, pause, pop, pause. They started to move as we came nearer. I heard a couple of pings on the window screen and saw a man at the back of one car aiming an air rifle. Rachael saw him and fired a volley into the car. The man ran for his life. I scraped the APC past the two cars. There was no one else in sight. I turned right and headed out of Ratby towards Kirby.

I could only do about twenty, so it was slow going. I called Nathan on the radio and asked if we were being followed. He replied that we were but at a distance. He told me he was firing at them when they got too close, so they backed off. Just to the left, in front of us, was a pub. I could see people in the road looking and pointing our way.

A car pulled across us into the road and stopped, the driver using it as a blockade. Even at a slow speed, the APC pushed through it. A few drops of blood hit the screen; not much, but someone must have been behind it when the APC hit. I didn't feel any remorse: they should have stayed out the way. Ahead was the mini roundabout for Desford Road. We were going straight over. It seemed clear, but as we passed, I saw cars to our right and again heard the faint 'ting' of air rifles.

Over the radio, I heard that someone had been hit. When I asked who it was, I was told it was Mary. I asked if she was alright. The reply came: no, she was hurt bad. We couldn't stop now. I told them to just get her as comfortable as possible.

Not forty metres ahead was the roundabout to Kirby. We were going straight on again. I tried to put my foot down, but the beast wouldn't go any faster. To the left I saw the castle; it looked unchanged. I wished it well and carried on.

I saw a plume of black smoke down the main road and saw the bin lorry racing up towards us. It would catch us easily at this speed, so I radioed the cars and lorry to make a run for it. With Rachael on the .50 cal, she might slow it down or even stop it with a well-placed round.

I looked in the mirror and saw the cars pull out to overtake. Off they went. The lorry was slower, and as it passed, Steve waved. I could see he wasn't happy that I made them go in the back. Rachael and Nathan sat there looking at me as they pulled away in the lorry. I saw Rachael put her arms around Nathan. I think she had started to cry.

My speed started to drop as we climbed the hill; in my mirrors I could see the bin lorry coming quickly behind me. I heard the .50 cal let loose, but it was still coming. It's hard to aim the gun in a moving vehicle; even harder when you shoot at a moving object.

The bin lorry started to lower its forks as it came nearer. I had the horrible feeling that it was going ram us, tipping us with the extensions. The firing above me stopped. After a couple of moments it started again. We were now at the top of the hill coming to another roundabout; we were going left. The lorry was only metres from the back of me, so I slowed right down and let Rachael get a good shot – she let loose another barrage.

The weapon stopped, and then there was banging on the roof. She popped her head down and shouted for me to go. I put my foot down and went. I couldn't see anything from my angle, then it came in view as I drove off. The front of the lorry's cab was gone, and it was off the road. She must have killed the driver.

Once off the roundabout, the road started to go downhill, and the APC picked up speed. We did another left, and another onto the A46. I was doing about forty as I came off the ring road onto the motorway. The bridge above was full of people. As we got nearer, they started to throw bricks and stones and fire their weapons at us.

I shouted through the back for Rachael to get into cover. She opened the cab hatch and smiled; "Already done babes." She kissed me and climbed into the passenger seat.

We were pelted with rubble, but the APC took it, and we drove on. We only went another mile before we pulled into the services to meet up with the others. I wanted to check on Mary, then get moving. If they saw us pull in, they might follow. Mary had been hit in the eye with a pellet; she had lost it. Paul had given her painkillers and covered her eye. She was asleep in the back seat. We went off, and at a very fast pace.

Chapter Eighteen

Mary was fast asleep on Josie's lap. Rose radioed through a sitrep for us. She moaned a little, but she was fine. What had happened was, when the convoy passed the Desford Road, a shotgun was fired at the car. It only took out the glass, but someone fired an air rifle and got lucky.

If we had been moving any slower at the farm, they may have got us all. Fortunately, until their main force arrived, Duncan's group stayed where they were. It was lucky we left when we did, another hour and they would have been swarming the house. Nathan called through and told us that just as we sped off, they saw at least a hundred people. He was sure he saw kids as well. How many of them died under Duncan's wrath? I tried not to worry for them. We drove in silence.

After leaving the services, I made the decision to go out of our way a bit. We travelled across on the M69, and then turned south on the A5, picking up the M1 at the M25. If Duncan did follow us, then I hoped he went straight down the M1. In their cars and vans, they would soon catch up to us, so I figured that going this way it made it safer.

We stopped at a hotel just off the junction for the A5. I wanted to make sure everyone was ok and get a bite to eat and drink before we moved on. The car park had a few roamers in it. Any that came too near got it in the head. Everyone was buzzing about the escape – they were all talking at once. I sat on a bench eating sausages and beans, watching a group of roamers.

"Rachael," said Paul, "What happened with the bin lorry? I thought you two were goners for a minute."

She told them that she was aiming for the engine block, just like I told her to, but it just didn't stop. She could see the rounds hitting, making a right mess of the front, but it kept on moving towards us. Once I'd slowed, she got a better aim and fired at the engine again, but still it came running. She changed her aim to the driver, taking him out in the fourth shot. One minute he had a head, then it was gone. When he died, he swerved into the hedge and crashed the lorry.

I told everyone the new route; we got out an atlas and planned stops on the way down. We were looking at places to stay, RVs and ERVs (rendezvous and emergency rendezvous). We also agreed to stock up on food and fuel whenever we could.

The group of dead I'd been watching had taken notice of us, so we packed away and drove off, leaving them behind.

That day's travel wasn't without events. A few villages we passed through seemed to be teeming with dead. The big APC pushed past them easily at first, but the thicker the crowd the harder it got. I was worried about jamming the wheels with bodies, and the cars would find it hard to pass over that many dead. We tried to go around them where we could, but it made the going slow.

By late afternoon we had made it to Milton Keynes. By staying on the old A5 Watling Road we got round quite easily. We had to find somewhere to stop – this was our first, planned overnight stay. Just after Bletchley, we saw a farm shop. It looked quiet, and it was fenced and gated. We went in and cleared the place.

We found three roamers. Once killed, we moved them to the back of the farm. The house was big: four bedrooms and two downstairs rooms. We had plenty of room to camp up. While Josie and Rose sorted dinner out, I took a party over the road to a petrol station to see what we could salvage.

A lot of the foodstuffs were out of date and had started to go mouldy. The fuel tanks were full, but we couldn't get the fuel out. The siphon wasn't long enough, and we dared not try to bucket it out without killing ourselves. We left it, but there were some gas canisters for the stoves – we took them. The farm shop was the same: any food had gone rotten, but we did find some full fuel cans that we added to our supply.

I wasn't sure what time it was when the scream woke me. I lay there in the dark, wondering if I'd dreamt it, and then I heard it again. It came from upstairs. I pushed my sleeping bag off and ran, grabbing my knife and gun on the way.

Others had been woken by the scream; there was panic and commotion on the landing. Paul called from one of the bedrooms, and when we ran in, the sight stunned us to silence.

In the middle of the room was Paul with his arms around Mary's body. She had turned and was gnashing at his face. Kelly went up to her and put her knife through Mary's temple. Paul let go and dropped her to the floor. I saw blood trickling down the side of his head. He put his hand to his ear, looked at the blood and swore. Mary had taken a bite out of his ear. Rose took Paul to the kitchen to clean the wound. We all followed, Emily put the kettle on and started to make tea and coffee.

As we sat and stood around the kitchen table, Rose and Paul told us what happened.

Paul and Rose slept in the same room as Mary, as Rose and Mary had become good friends. Rose had woken in the night to go to the toilet and had checked on Mary, who was still asleep. So she went back to bed. She was nodding off again when she heard a noise. When she opened her eyes, there was a shape floating in front of her. Shocked and groggy, she sat up to get a better look. Mary was hanging from the ceiling light.

Rose's scream woke people up; Paul shot out of bed. In a daze, he looked over at Rose. She was still screaming, pointing at the body hanging there. He went for his knife, righted the chair Mary had used and cut her down. She didn't fall to the floor: she landed on her feet and stood there, swaying.

As Paul got off the chair, he slipped, dropping his knife. Mary went for him – all he could do was to hold her down until someone came to help. Rose was crying, curled up on the bed. Hearing that other people had woken up, Paul called for help.

I looked around the room and realised not everyone was there. Neave was still asleep; Jason wasn't there and neither was my Rachael. Everyone sat in silence, consumed by their own thoughts. A question was on everyone's mind, but they dare not ask.

Paul got up from the table and said he was going for a walk. Everyone watched him go then turned to me as he left. I got up and followed him out.

"And where do you think you're going?" I said, quickening my pace to catch up with him.

"I need time to think," he replied, "you can't cut my ear off to save me this time."

"I know."

He turned to me and I saw he had a gun in his hand.

"You're not topping yourself," I insisted, "we'll stand by you – there might be a cure in London. It was only a small bite, it may be days before you ... you know, turn." I looked at him and him at me.

"I wish I knew you before all this," he said, "I think we would have been really good friends."

"We are good friends, Paul, you've been my right hand man."

He lifted his hand and laughed.

"Nick, I've grown to love you as a friend, even a brother, but I can't wait. Say goodbye to everyone for me."

He put the gun to his head. Before I could stop him, he pulled the trigger.

The gun jammed. Paul looked at me and pulled the trigger again – nothing. I grabbed his hand, took the gun off him and punched him in the face. He went down.

"You fucking twat!" I shouted. "I'm not having two suicides in one night. Say your own fucking goodbyes, not me. Now get in there and be the man I respect, and we'll get through this."

He got to his knees and started to cry, "Nick, I don't want to be one of them; please kill me before it happens, please ..." he wailed.

I went to him, picked him up and gave him a hug. The last time I hugged a man was my dad, before he died, and then I felt uncomfortable. This was different, Paul was a man who I cared for and respected.

We walked around for a while to help clear his head. When we got back to the kitchen, most had gone back to bed; it was just Rose and Josie waiting.

Rose had a worried look on her face. She got up, hugging and kissing him. "You silly man," she said and kissed him again. They went off to bed – maybe they were going to talk.

"Is he alright?" asked Josie.

"No, he's not, but we'll get him through this."

When I got to the living room, Rachael was up, as was Jess. Jason was on the floor near Neave, asleep. My face must have asked the question I was thinking. He was supposed to be in with Tony and Jayne.

"He watched over her when everyone went upstairs," said

Rachael. "I saw him come down here, so I followed. He was just looking at her sleeping. When I walked in he cried and said sorry for being an idiot. So we sat together while everything else was going on."

Jess looked over at him, she was still cold.

Breakfast was a quiet affair between Mary's death and Paul's injury. We had just started to pack the cars when Jason asked to speak to me. I walked him over to the petrol station.

"I want a job here. You saved my life, and I'm grateful, but I feel you don't trust me." He paused, I stayed quiet. "I know I've got to prove myself – please take me out on a supply run, and I'll show you I can be trusted."

"Anything else?" I asked. I was waiting for him to ask for a gun. If he did it would make up my mind.

"Not really, but ..." *Here it comes*, I thought. "I would like to learn to drive, so I could help with the runs."

That was different to a gun, but I was still suspicious: he may have wanted to make a run for it. Then he could go back and tell Duncan where we were.

"I'll think about it, but until then you stay with Tony."

He seemed to want to say something else. Eventually he did, "Can you ask Jess if I can spend some time with Neave? I miss her, and I just want to look after her a bit."

"I'll see. Just keep your nose clean and do as we say. I'll think about what you've asked."

We went back to the farm; everyone was ready and just waiting for us. We got into our vehicles and left.

Chapter Nineteen

The A5 was a nice road to drive down. Back in the day, it would have been quite busy, but now it was a quiet drive in the countryside. We saw the odd dead moving about. We just drove past them.

When we came to Dunstable, we hit more of the beasts. I tried to drive through them, but Paul radioed in to say it was tough going for the cars. They had to drive around the bodies – the moving dead started to swarm them. We decided to U-turn and make our way around Dunstable rather than go through it.

The road was too narrow for the lorry and APC. We went down a side street to go around the block and head back the way we came. There were more dead, so Rachael and Kelly started to shoot them. We didn't want them overpowering us.

The dead they cut down ended up blocking the road. The cars were still having trouble, so we had to get out and clear it. Tony and Jayne covered our backs while we moved the bodies. Rachael and Kelly stayed on the guns to cover the front. The rest of us moved the bodies to the side.

I could hear gunfire from the rear, so we must have been attracting more. I told Tom to drive the APC forward so we could move on. Rachael and Kelly started to fire when a crowd of roamers came around the corner. I was proud of the girls: they were firing in small bursts and hitting their marks.

We had to move the bodies quickly. The firing went quiet. When I looked back, I saw both Rachael and Kelly reloading their guns. They were moving as fast as they could, but it was wasted time – more roamers came on. I took out my pistol and started to fire at the dead as they moved ever closer.

I had to reload twice before the big guns started up again, but the dead were too close. It turned into hand-to-hand combat. I ordered everyone back to the cars and lorry for cover. At the front were Paul, Jason and Steve who had gotten out of the lorry. Rose, Jess and I joined them, while Nathan and Rachael Two covered the cars – Neave, Emily, Josie and Flo were still in them.

I told everybody to move back again, but Paul told me to shut up and fight. I could hear the gunfire at the back, so we still had more of them coming from the rear. Between a rock and a hard place came to mind. I thought: *how in hell are we going to fight off this many roamers?*

I ordered people to get the assault rifles; they went one at a time. I told them to shoot at the legs – it would slow them down, buy us a minute. The two bigger guns were aiming at the back of the crowd, as they didn't want to hit us.

We started to spray the dead with bullets. The ones behind tripped over the fallen. I called to Steve and Jason to take out the ones that were down. It seemed to work, the roamers on their feet were slowed, though some went around the side, so we dealt with them.

Flo tapped me on the shoulder and handed me more magazines for my rifle. She picked up the spent one and went to the next person, doing the same. She must have gotten out of the car to help, as did Josie. She then went to the back of the APC and loaded the empties.

As I watched, I saw Emily with Neave in the back of the nearest car. I could see the fear on Emily's face, but she was holding it together for Neave's sake. The child was crying with the noise.

A scream made me turn back. Josie was covered in roamers. I saw one take a chunk out of her neck, blood spurted over the dead and drove them into a frenzy. I raised my rifle and fired into the group, putting a hole in Josie's head – it was the best for her. The beasts fell to the ground as I fired more rounds into them. Steve came running over to see if he could help. I shook my head: we would mourn her later.

I turned back to the battle just as Paul ran into the swarm, spraying them with fire. He even used the rifle has a club; he wanted to die fighting, so I let him. I didn't want him to go, but I knew he had little time left. Fighting to the death was the best thing for him, he would die a hero.

The bodies were starting to pile up: Jason was killing the ones on the ground with my sword. Every now and again he took a swing at one still standing. He was covered, head to foot, in blood and guts. I saw Paul at the back of them, taking them down with his hook and knife. He had run out of ammo, so he was fighting physically. I saw a roamer coming from behind him. I took aim, but its head exploded before I pulled the trigger. I turned and saw Rachael grinning, and then she carried on firing.

The swarm was starting to thin out, but we still couldn't move – there were too many bodies blocking our way. I went to the back and saw that it wasn't as bad; from their high point, Tony and Jayne were safe. I fired into the small crowd and went to have a look around the corner. It wasn't that blocked, but the cars wouldn't make it.

I ran to the front and told Tom to start moving forward again – and to put his foot down when I gave him the signal. I told Jess to get Rachael Two, Nathan, Neave and Emily and get them into the APC. I told Jason and Rose to make their way to the APC as well. Steve: I told him to get the lorry started and back out off the road. I told him to meet us at the junction of the next street.

I waved to Tom, and the APC roared forward, bouncing its way over the dead bodies. I ran after it, and when I got to Paul, I dragged him along. Once past the worst of it, Tom stopped and waited till Paul and I climbed in. Off we roared.

I worked my way to the front of the cab, it was a tight squeeze. I told Tom to go the way we came into Dunstable and keep going for about two miles. Once we turned out of the road, the lorry followed.

We found a quiet place to stop and work out how to get around Dunstable. With us all looking at the map, we figured that we would have to go miles out of our way to get back on track. So we did.

Two hours later, we were back on the A5. We stopped at a petrol station for a break. Everyone was tired and worn out. There was no sign of any dead around, so we relaxed a bit and had something to eat and drink. We made it our camp for the night. Luckily, we put some tents into the lorry, as most of the sleeping bags were in the cars. It was a cold night.

Chapter Twenty

The next morning was a quiet affair, everyone thinking about Josie. I had told them what happened and how she went. We ate our breakfast in silence. I went over to Paul to see how he was doing.

"You fought hard yesterday," I said, "can anything kill you?"

He laughed, "Well, you can't say I didn't try." He lowered his head and whispered, "Got bit again ..." He pulled up his trouser leg, and I saw the teeth marks on his shin, but the skin wasn't broken. "The thing is, Nick," he paused, "I feel great. I remember when Keith died: it only took a few hours. I'm into my second day, and I feel I could fight the world."

I couldn't believe what he had just told me. Yes, Keith had only taken hours, and he died in his sleep. I stared at Paul's face and could see small veins showing in his cheeks and neck.

"What you staring at?" he asked.

I told him what I could see; I thought that it was part of the infection. We sat in silence for a few minutes.

"But I should be dead, what if I'm immune?"

"What if ... when we chopped your hand off, a tiny amount of the virus got into you, and your body's antibodies fought it and succeeded? What if it made you resilient to the virus, so when Mary took your ear off, your body wasn't affected because you already are?"

"You mean I'm not going to die?" he sounded astonished.

"Well, yeah. I'm not *too* sure, you still may do, but you *should* be out for the count *now* or at least weak as a kitten."

He gave a mighty roar which made the others look over at us. We stood up and went over to tell them our theory. Rose jumped up and kissed him. Everyone was patting him on the back, and it seemed to cheer the group up.

I went over to Jason and told him to follow me. He was looking strained and tired. I took him round the back of the station and sat him down against the wall.

"I saw you yesterday, fighting them things without even a moan. You just waded into them and took them out."

He stopped looking so scared and seemed surprised.

"It was either them or us," he said.

I paused a second then finally said, "You've just made my mind up as to what I'm going to do with you." I took my pistol out. A look of total fear came across his face – I tried my best not to laugh.

"You have got to learn how to use this properly," I ejected the mag, turned the gun, holding it by the barrel, and handed it to him. He took it gently, looked at it, then at me.

"Are you sure?" he asked. "I know I have to work hard, but I've only been with you less than a week."

"You proved you can fight and stand on your own two feet, plus you've said the right things. If you had said, 'them or me', I wouldn't be giving you this. Also you've not asked to have a gun, so I think it's time."

He gave me a smile.

"I've been a pig-headed fool. You have always tried to help me in the past, and I've thrown it back in your face. This last year has made me grow up. I'll do anything you say and follow your example." He had a tear in the corner of his eye; he wiped it and said, "Damn dust."

121

"You have, and I'm still watching you. I'll talk to Jess, but you'll see lot of Neave now, as you'll be in the same vehicle. Now get back there and I'll show you how to use it, come on."

With that, he stood up, and we walked around to the far side of the building. I showed him the ropes.

At breakfast, I sat looking at the map and followed the A5 down toward the M25. There was a town called St Albans between us and there. With the trouble in Dunstable, I wondered if we should get back on the motorway as soon as possible. We would pass right under St Albans in a few miles.

I went over to the group and asked their opinion. They more or less said that what I said went. They simply trusted my judgement and would follow. I felt humbled again: these people were now my family, not just people off the street.

We stopped again, just before we hit the motorway, at a service station. We needed to refuel the lorry and APC. There was a hotel opposite and a lot of cars in the car park, so we went off to find some keys. We would have to enter the hotel and search the rooms. We agreed to only do the ground floor, and as soon as we found three sets of keys we'd check out the cars and get moving. I wanted to hit the edge of London before nightfall, camp up and rest before the big push.

I was surprised: there weren't many roamers about, but I was thankful for small mercies. I told the group to collect blankets and pillows, as ours were lost in the cars. We also raided the kitchen and found loads of tinned goods. This place must have had a delivery just before the outbreak.

Jason, Nathan, Paul, Tony and I checked the rooms, and we each found a set of car keys. Tony was happy – he found a set for an Aston Martin and couldn't wait to find it and try it out. We went out into the car park and found our respective cars. Only one started, which was an old Ford Escort; it had been lovingly cared for. We got a set of jump leads from the garage and jumpstarted the others. Tony drove around the car park in the Aston, but then we all had a go. I took Jason for a spin. I scared the crap out of him, doing escape manoeuvres, wheel spinning and handbrake turns. I even did a full speed reverse with a J-turn.

In the end we picked the Escort; I wanted to teach Jason to drive in it. We also took a Citroën C5 estate and a BMW. We started to load the cars with food and blankets. By the time we had done everything, it was well past midday. We decided to stay for the night, using the hotel to sleep in. We kept to the ground floor, blocking off stairwells so we wouldn't have any uninvited guests. We each picked a room for the night, but I did insist on a guard outside.

The rest of the day was a nice change from the day before. We saw no more roamers after we dispatched the few that were around. At the back of the hotel was a children's playground; we all sat around there watching Neave playing and laughing. I wondered if any of this new world would scar her. We tried to keep her away from the horrors we faced, but, like yesterday, she saw the full force of it. Someone she knew had even died. At this moment, she seemed happy to be pushed on the swings by her mother, who was also laughing.

I looked over at Jason who was looking rather sad. I could tell he wanted to go over. I tried to catch Jess's attention, pointing over to Jason and giving a shrug. She softly nodded and called him over to have a go. His face lit up, and he nearly tripped over, which made a lot of us laugh.

When he got to Neave, she told him to push her hard, as mummy wouldn't. He went for it; they were laughing so hard that he started to get tears in his eyes. Jess came over and sat next to me. She hooked her arm in mine and put her head on my shoulder. I put my head on hers and told her that I loved her. She replied with the same.

"What about you two?" I asked.

"I don't love him anymore. I missed him to start with, but when I thought he was dead I got over him. I know he's changed, but so have I. He can see and play with Neave when he wants, but him and me? No, we're finished."

"Have you told him yet?"

"No, I don't know how. We've been through so much the last week ..." she stopped.

"Okay, babes, but you must tell him soon: why not tonight? I'll put both of you on guard, and you can talk it through."

She nodded into my shoulder, and we just sat and watched.

After we had dinner, I tasked the guard for the night and got Paul and Nathan to siphon as much fuel from the cars as they could. They filled eight jerrycans. Once they were stowed away, we all turned in for the night. I put Jess and Jason on first so they could talk. It was only a two-hour rota, so everyone got a good night's sleep.

Chapter Twenty-One

Everyone seemed happy the next morning. Dunstable seemed to have never happened. We had learnt over the last year not to dwell on the bad. If you did, it would drive you insane. Just before we had breakfast, I took Jason for a quick lesson around the car park, then up and down the road. He took to it quite well. I told him that once we were on the motorway, and if it was quiet, I'd let him take over. We headed back to the hotel and got ready for the off.

The vehicles started up, and we left for the last leg before London. Tom and Flo were in the APC. Next were Paul, Rose, Neave and Jess. Then it was me with Jason, Rachael and Emily. In the last car were Tony and Jayne, with Rachael Two and Nathan. Steve and Kelly were at the back driving the lorry.

The motorway had a lot of abandoned vehicles – lorries, cars, buses, vans, they were all there – we had to weave in and around them. It was slow going, but I noticed something: there were a lot of dead people in the cars, not moving. They were dead, actually dead. I wanted to check it out, but everyone else wanted to keep moving, so we did.

Every now and again, we would stop and check the road ahead. Tony, Steve and I would stand on top of the APC, looking through binoculars. We could see for miles. Once in a while, we would see a couple of roamers. It didn't worry us too much. We knew it was safe to go on without mounting the big guns.

On one of these stops, I swapped places with Jason, and

he drove for some time. He was a little nervous, manoeuvring around the stationary vehicles, but he did well and soon mastered the art. I asked him about Jess.

He was quiet then said: "We're over; I thought we would be. It was my fault in the first place, being so big-headed and knowing best. I told her I'd changed, but she wasn't having any of it." He paused, then carried on, "She did say I'm allowed around Neave and can have her anytime. I would love to stay a family, but we have to move on." I got the impression that he wanted to say no more, so I let it be.

While Jason was driving, I managed to get a good look at the dead in the cars. None of the windows were smashed, and the bodies were dried-out husks. How was it that these people were dead and had not turned? Was it like this all the way to London or just in this area?

After about ten miles, the cars started to thin out, and the driving was faster. I saw a sign for services in sixteen miles and for the M25 in six. I decided that we may as well stop there, then travel into London the next day. We still stopped for a recce when we could. We could see miles ahead and it was all clear. I asked Paul about the bodies in the cars – he never noticed, but he was driving at the time.

We got to the services by late afternoon and there were loads of lorries. We siphoned them off and refuelled the vehicles. There were quite a few dead roaming, so we went off in small parties to get rid of them. Paul's group came back, all covered in blood, and said that there was a hotel farther down. They had cleared the ground floor; we could have proper beds again tonight.

We drove the vehicles over and parked them at the front, ready to move out. We had another cold dinner before turning in for the night. We put the guards out on overnight watch and hit the sack, ready for tomorrow.

Chapter Twenty-Two

I was just about to go out and call in the guard for breakfast when Tony came running in. His face was grey, and when he saw me, all he could do was point. I looked in the direction, shaking my head in wonder when he said, "They're dead!"

"Who are?" I asked.

"Nathan and Rachael," he replied, "throats cut and holes in their heads!"

I ran to the APC and lorry: both had been emptied. I stood there looking at the scene. Blood ran down the front and sides of the APC. The two bodies lay on the floor as if they had been thrown from the top. People started to turn up –

Tony must have told them in the dining room, and they came to see.

I couldn't take my eyes off the bodies of these two young people, new to our group. They worked hard to become part of our family, and now lay on the floor, taken from us. My temper started to rise: I wanted to punish the scum that did this. That's when a thought hit me. I turned around, scanned the area and then looked at my group. I was the only one carrying my pistol and knife. My rifle was back in the dining room.

"Get your fucking weapons!" I barked. "They may still be here!"

Everyone double looked, then ran back to the hotel. That's when I heard the shot. I ran back with them to collect my rifle. We had no ammunition, only the magazines we carried. All I knew about the other group was that they had two rifles and two pistols – but they had a shit load of ammo. Luckily, we'd taken the .50 cal and the machine gun in to clean. Their ammo was in the lorry and APC, though, so they were useless.

Everyone gathered in the reception area with their weapons, all were ready to fight. Emily was the only one not there, she had taken Neave to her room. This was the plan if anything ever happened: everyone was to stand to, and she would take Neave to a safe place. I had to think of something fast; we could all get killed here and now. I didn't know how many there were outside, all I knew was their weapons loadout.

"Right, block the main doors, I want us on the top floor. We can defend from there."

"We'll need to clear each floor on the way up," said Tony.

"No, just the stairwell, but as we pass each floor, I want the doors open to let any dead in. Then they will have to work past them to get to us."

Right, it was a plan. Jess went to fetch Neave and Emily.

Paul and Tony went ahead. Once on the first floor, they called 'all clear', and the group went up. At the back were Steve, Kelly and myself. We waited until the second floor was clear, then we went up, opened and wedged the door and waited till the top floor was safe. I had instructed the group to clear every room and not to shoot unless they had to.

Ten long minutes later, the all clear was called. We moved to the second floor and did the same with the door. Once on the top floor, I told Steve and Kelly to watch the stairwell door. I went to Paul and told him to wedge open all the internal doors; we needed to be able to move around and communicate. The only door which was left shut was the one with Neave and Emily inside.

I went from window to window, seeing if I could spot

anything. As I did, I placed someone at each to watch for movement. They were to call out when they saw anything. We had four magazines each, giving each person about 120 rounds. From our high position, we could defend easily if we took aim and were observant. They could spray our position and hit someone, but they had to shoot up, and that's harder than shooting down. I was in no mood to talk our way out of this – I wanted them dead.

Twenty minutes later, Tom shouted that he could see movement in the trees.

"If you see anybody, you shoot to kill. They will kill us if they can," I shouted.

There was no reply. Only Rachael One, Nathan (God rest his soul) and I had killed a living person. I was asking a lot from these people, but they saw what happened to Rachael Two and Nathan, still lying out there.

I heard a shot; I listened for another and tried to work out where it came from. *Was it Tom?* Then, from outside, rapid shots were fired and glass started breaking. I shouted, asking if it was Tom's area. Tom replied with an 'affirmative'. I then saw movement in front of me, and a burst of fire lanced my way.

I looked through my sights: it was a man. He just stood there like Rambo, firing from the hip – *twat*. I looked over my rifle's sights, guessed the distance and fired twice. One hit him in the chest, the other in the neck. The man dropped to the floor. With my eye on the rifle in his hand, I waited. A kid no more than nineteen went to pick it up. I put a round through his head. He dropped.

I was hearing fire from all over the floor by this time. I was glad it was all single burst. Looking to my left and right, people were moving towards the hotel. Every now and then a shot was fired and an enemy dropped. I had taught my people well.

Another man came for the rifle, I shot him. I looked over my sights and saw twenty-odd people moving slowly towards us, flitting between cover. I shouted to Tony, who was at the back, asking how many he could see. He said about twenty. That was forty in total.

Back on my side of the building, I saw three drop. I took another two out. I was just covering the dropped rifle. Someone else came forward, a woman this time. She kept looking back; I heard a shout but couldn't see who it was. She was looking at the hotel, then back. I called out to the floor not to shoot at her – I had the rifle covered. I heard more shots from the back.

I fired just in front of her. She stopped and looked up; through my sights I could see she was scared. Another shout: she moved closer. I fired again. She started to cry, and a pool of water formed at her feet. She had just pissed herself. I leaned out of the window and shouted for the group to back off. I called Jess and Rachael, they came running in.

Without turning to them I said: "Get down to the front doors and shut the other floors down. That girl is going to die if we don't save her. Take Paul with you."

Without a word they ran off, calling Paul as they went.

"You girl, get to the front doors now. Someone will meet you," I shouted down, out the window.

She looked back at her group – the person shouted something I couldn't hear. She looked back at me and ran to the doors. A man ran towards the rifle; I took him down.

I shouted for the leader to go for it. A large man stepped from behind a wall. He was holding a girl in front of him with a pistol to her head. Through the sights I could see fear on her face; she was crying.

The rest of his gang started to move away. He came slowly forward, moving towards the rifle. I fired a shot in front of it

– he stopped and looked up. I suddenly realised that my group had stopped firing.

I scanned the interlopers: they were afraid of this man. *Would they leave him if they could?*

I was back on him; his left shoulder was open. I took a deep breath and fired one shot. He let go of the girl, who ran back to her people. A young man took her, holding her and kissing her head.

The leader stood up, clutching his shoulder, and shouted at her to get back. She stayed in the arms of the man, her group closing in around her. The leader walked up, aimed at the man protecting her and shot him in the face.

I put a bullet through the leader's head, dropping him like a stone. The rest backed away and put their hands up. The hostiles from the back of the hotel came round the corner with their hands up.

Tony came in, telling me that the enemy simply gave up after he and the others had killed about ten of them. When they heard me shouting, they went around the corner to surrender. I called out for people to stay at their windows, and watch for more movement.

I took Tony with me downstairs. As we went, I saw dead roamers in the stairwell, so there were some about. When we got to the reception area, Jess had the girl tied to a chair. The girl was still crying – I felt it was through stress and not from being bound. No one held a gun to her. Going to the front doors, I went outside, and the opposing force stood in front of me, all hands raised. I looked for the biggest man and went over to him. This was something I was taught in the army: take the biggest out first and show your dominance. His face was covered in scars, some of them fresh. I looked into his eyes and saw fear.

"Who are you, and where do you come from?"

"We are just survivors, like you. We got mixed up with this nutter – he was good to us at first, fed us and let us join his gang. He said he would keep us safe. Then he started to cut me," he raised a hand to his cheek, "just because I questioned his motives." He turned to the group, looking for support.

This sounded familiar. It couldn't be, though, not after more than a week? It seemed that they had come after us, finding us to boot.

"Where's Duncan?" I asked.

"You know him?"

"We're the ones he's been looking for the past week."

"Honest, buddy, I didn't know – we were picked up near Lutterworth."

"So you followed this man and did his bidding?"

"Look man, he's got my daughter, if we don't return with you people he will kill her."

"Where is he?"

"At this place near Elstree."

I looked at the other people, they seemed relieved we weren't go to kill them. I had a quick count: there were fifteen.

"How many are left there, at Elstree?"

He turned to the group, some of them shrugged. "About another twenty, I reckon."

"How many henchmen does he have left?"

Something caught my eye: it was the girl who was held by the leader. I tried not to look at her; she was shaking her head, her eyes bored into mine.

I turned back to the big guy, "If you're lying to me, I will kill you."

"No, man, I'm not! I promise: there's about four of them. I know one is guarding the hostages, and he's been told to kill them if anything happens."

I let it be. Without turning, I called my group out. Moments later, Paul came up behind me, so I knew they were there.

I told the group in front of me to sit down. I went to the dead people and picked up the rifle and the pistol.

"If any move, shoot them." I went to Tony and told him to fetch the other rifle and pistol.

"One last question, where's our stuff?"

"Over by the yard, back there," he pointed over his shoulder.

I knew where he meant. "Anyone looking after it?"

"No."

I went to the girl: "You follow me."

She got up and followed me back to the reception. Once inside, I told Jess to untie the first girl.

"Names," I ordered.

The first girl was Kim, and the second was Sally.

"Sally, what do you want to say?"

"He's lying about the numbers and the stores. There are three people watching your stuff. And back at the camp site, he has about forty people and six henchmen left. But he was telling the truth about his daughter. Others have children being held hostage too."

"Is there a plan for the return? How were you supposed to bring us back?"

"I don't know, the boss man knew the plans. We were just told to fight and get the stuff."

"Who killed my two people last night?"

"Mr Taylor, the one with the gun. He's the one who slashed Jackson's face."

"Will Jackson help me get my stuff back and kill Duncan?"

"I'm not sure, because of his daughter ..."

"Right." I needed time to think. "When is Duncan expecting you back?"

"I think I heard Mr Taylor talking to Mr Martin, something about two days."

"Right," my brain went into overdrive. We needed a plan, but first I needed to get our stuff back.

Chapter Twenty-Three

We started to work out how we were going to help set these people free from a tyrant. We went over to the service yard, where they kept the minibuses and our stores. I told Jackson what the girls had said. I assured him I would get Duncan's hostages back. I had to trust that he would go along with the plan – we would need him if it was to have a chance. The three who were on guard had to be taken out first: they were in league with Duncan.

Jackson and I went to the service yard with some members of each of our groups. I kept my hands behind me.

As we came into view, the two saw us coming and held up their air rifles. I smiled to myself.

"Its okay, man," shouted Jackson, "we've got the son of a bitch." He gave me a shove.

"Where's Mr Taylor?"

"Took a bullet," said Jackson.

"Wow, can't believe you've got him!" said one, walking towards us.

"Heard a lot of firing; thought you'd had it," said the other, walking alongside.

They lowered the rifles, and as we got closer, I shot both of them in the head with two double taps. I turned to the third and double tapped him as he was raising his rifle. We walked by them, not even looking, and went to get our stuff. Paul called on the radio to bring the lorry and APC round so we could reload them.

Once the stuff was loaded, we went back to the hotel. Kelly and Steve cleared the first floor. We put our prisoners/guests into the rooms. We told them that no one was to leave until we came for them. I asked Sally and Kim: who could be trusted within their group? Kim said a man called Scott was her boyfriend, and that he was a good person. When I asked why, she told me he had stopped one of the henchmen raping her, and was nearly hanged for the deed. Instead, he was whipped until he passed out. I needed Jackson, as he had the look of a big, bad man; my gut sort of trusted him. He seemed to have something about him. He stood up to Duncan and got punished, so he could be a man to have at your side. My only worry: with his daughter in danger, how far would he go to save her? He might even betray us to ensure her safety.

I went upstairs and called out for Scott. A young man of about twenty five came out, looking very nervous. I asked him if he knew where Duncan's camp was and if he could read a map. Since satnav became popular, a lot of people had lost the ability to read one. I needed to know if he could show me on the roadmap where it was. He said he knew how to get to it but was not sure about the map.

I took him downstairs and showed him where we were, where Elstree was and talked him through the roads around the area. By working back from the services, we at last found the site. It was times like this that I wish I had an ordinance survey map – it would have shown me the lay of the land: wooded areas, hills, terrain. I remembered that there was a WH Smiths at the services, but it would mean getting by any new roamers that had turned up. We still had the odd one wander through, even though we cleared the area. I told Scott to wait, while I went to the manager's office. How I could have kissed him – he had a local A-Z and an ordinance survey.

Back in the dining room, I showed Scott the map and asked if he knew anything of the area. Specifically, I wanted to know where any lookouts were posted. He looked at it, and his face was blank. He shook his head, so I thanked him for his help and sent him back to his room. I wanted to ask Jackson, but at that moment I dared not.

I wanted to go and recce the area before we attacked it. I called for a volunteer to go with me for cover while I checked it out. They all wanted to go; I chose Steve. I sat down with him in the manager's office and talked through the plan of action.

We lay up in a wooded area at the back of the complex that was home to Duncan and his gang. Both Steve and I were covered in guts so as not to attract any roamers. We also wore black cloths we had found in the hotel.

I could see a large building to the right, and to the left, a smaller complex with some houses. It was at the houses where a lot of movement was going on. There were seven semi-detached homes. By the layout of the guards, the middle house must have been where the hostages were held. I pulled a notepad out of my pocket and drew a detailed map of the area. After two hours of watching, I saw no sign of Duncan. My prisoners at the hotel would be able to tell me where with the help of the map.

We slowly left the wood and made our way back to the services and hotel, killing a couple of roamers and using them for gut suits. Once back, I told Steve to have a break and get cleaned up. I got myself cleaned up and called the group into the dining room. We put the plan of action forward, ironing out any kinks as we went.

Two hours later, everything was agreed. We all had tasks to do to ready for the attack. I went to the first floor and called everyone into the corridor. I asked who had family or loved ones held hostage back at Duncan's site. Six people came forward, including Jackson. I took them upstairs into an empty room and spoke to them.

"Right, I've been and done a recce at your site, and I could see where your families were being held hostage." I looked at each person in turn and could tell they were worried.

"Tomorrow, before first light, we are going to attack the complex. You lot, along with me, are going to rescue the families." I paused, and no one said anything. I looked at Jackson – his brain was in overdrive. "The others are going to cause a diversion while we go into the hostage house, kill the guards and get your families out."

"How are they going to cause the diversion?" asked a woman.

"And your name is?"

"Jill, they have my sons in there."

"Jill, the diversion is not your problem. We have radios; once we are in place, we will call the other group and keep coordinated. Then we'll go in before anyone can be hurt." I said with a tone that shocked her.

I continued: "Do any of you know where in the house the hostages are being kept?"

A couple thought that they may be kept in an upstairs bedroom, maybe one at the back of the house.

"Alright then, back to your rooms, and don't say anything to the others just yet. I've got to brief them on what they are doing."

This seemed to cheer them up – the news that we had a good plan and were willing to help them. To me these people weren't the problem, it was Duncan. He wanted to rule the world and would do anything to get it.

"Oh, just one more thing, I need to know where Duncan hides, because once your people are free, we're going after him."

After I briefed the rest of the prisoners on their part of the plan, I told them to rest and get ready for an early start. The rest of us prepared for the attack, cleaning weapons, making sure the vehicles were serviced, and I taught Jason how to drive the APC. We emptied the lorry again, then stored the stuff in a secure place. We'd need it to transport the people we rescued back.

I brought everyone down to the dining room, my people and the new, for one final talk before everyone went to bed.

"Tomorrow is going to be dangerous. Some of us may get killed in the fighting." The room was a hush; every single pair of eyes was looking at me. I looked at every person and to my friends; a nod was given and returned.

"If you stay with your group leader and do what is asked, you will survive. I want no heroics. If you see something, tell your leader, and they will make the decision." Again the room was quiet. The heat from the bodies made it warm.

"We can do this, and we will, now go to bed and get rest, take food if you need it," Flo had laid a table full of food. People got up, got something to eat then went to bed.

As I lay next to Rachael, I could hear her breathing rhythmically. She was asleep. My thoughts were on these new people: why should we help them? We had our own agenda, and I still wanted to go through with it. But Duncan was a tyrant. He wanted my people and me dead, so we had to stop him. They just fell unlucky to meet him; but they would have killed us if they weren't stopped. But they *were* stopped, and their true light came to the front. We had to help them. We had the guns, and now the people. It could be done.

Chapter Twenty-Four

We lay in the bushes opposite the hostage house. When we got to the site, we found a two-metre high metal fence along the compound side. It had nasty, pointed tops. I told my group to wait while I checked out farther down. To my luck, there was a car park that led to the houses from the other way.

Because it was pitch black, we could move in closer without being seen. It was hard to tell if there was a guard on the house – it was so dark. Then I saw a cigarette being lit; the man was on his own. I wondered how many guards were on the inside, as no one was sure back at the briefing. I felt very sure that, with most of the force gone, it wouldn't be many.

I radioed through: we were in position. No reply came for a moment and then Jess said they were ready. Two minutes later Steve said he was ready, and then straight away Tony came through.

Each group knew to radio in order, as not to get confused. It was me first, then Jess and Paul with their group, then it would be Steve and Kelly, and last were Tony and Jayne. Jason was with Rachael in the APC, and in the lorry were Tom and Emily. They were about two-miles away, and once they heard the noise they were to come in with the big guns blazing. Back at the hotel, Flo stayed with Neave. We would wait till first light, then I would give the order to start the attack. I didn't want us shooting at our own side, so we waited, which wasn't too long.

"Stand by. Stand by," I said into the radio, and paused for a final check. "Go, go, go," I ordered. I put away the radio and aimed my rifle at the guard.

Somewhere behind our position I heard gunfire and a lot of shouting. The guard dropped his cigarette and turned towards the house. I double tapped him in the head. A face came to a top-floor window, mouthed something and disappeared. I ordered my group to go. We ran to the door; I held my rifle to the shoulder, so it was in position at all times. Just as we got to it, it opened – standing there was a young man with a pistol. I fired two shots into his head. I went into the house first, heading straight upstairs. Half the group followed me, the rest cleared the inside.

At the top, I checked the landing, calling, "Clear." I went to the back of the house and stood at a bedroom door, listening, while the rest checked the other rooms. A woman called Julie ran past me, quickly pushing the door open. In the room in front of me were the hostages, and behind them, a man with short hair and a long beard. He held a knife to the throat of a young girl; she was no more than ten. I double tapped him and the girl screamed, running to Julie, her mother.

The rest of my group came up, and the parents were reunited with their children. They thanked me; Jackson shook my hand and apologized for lying. I told him not to mention it. Then I told everyone to stay where they were until our transport arrived.

As I left the house, I could still hear gunfire, but in this area it was quiet. I wondered if the noise would draw roamers to us. We would just have to deal with that when the time came. I radioed Tom to come and fetch the hostages, telling him where to find them; he came back with a, "Roger that."

I could hear the .50 cal firing by now, giving the group cover

141

from the back. We should have them circled by this point – our three groups at the front, and the APC at the back. I wanted to find Duncan. Would he be with his forces, or would he be hiding? I had to find out. I made my way to the APC, killing a couple of roamers on the way.

I looked over the field: it was quite light now, and I could see where the battle had been fought. I could also see a small pocket of hand-to-hand fighting. It was short lived: Tony, with his rifle as motivation, called them to stop.

There were dead bodies on the ground, but I couldn't tell if they were ours or theirs. I found out later it was mostly theirs; only four of ours had died. None of my original group were injured, though Paul had tripped over and gotten stampeded by his own team. It seemed our firepower and numbers won the day. Rounding up the survivors, we herded them into a small group. Everyone with a gun covered them.

By the time I got to them, everything was under control. There were eight left of the original forty. I looked at each one – none were Duncan, though a couple had a look of defiance on them. I turned back to the battlefield and saw a couple of bodies twitching. I went over to Paul and asked him to take care of any that turned. Off he went, taking out his pistol, reloading to carry on.

Back to the prisoners: I asked where Duncan was. No one replied. I went to one of my new people, a man called Dexter, and gave him my pistol. I told him to shoot one of Duncan's lieutenants. He walked up to one man who looked angry. As Dexter got closer, the man told him he was going to be hanged for his treason. Dexter pointed the gun and fired. The lieutenant died.

I asked the question again. The rest of the prisoners started to talk at once, some pleading, others giving answers. Dexter walked over to another large man who was pleading for his life – he was even crying. Dexter said that he wasn't so brave now. I told Dexter to stop, and then told the big man to stand. Everyone went quiet and looked at him.

I again asked the question: "Where's Duncan?"

"He's over the road, there's a big house. He lives there with his wives."

"How many guard him?"

"Normally Five, but we all came out here when we heard the noise."

"What is he doing now?"

"Probably waiting for one of us to go back and report to him."

"So, he's not worried that you would lose?"

"No, why should he be? There are a lot of us."

"Were. There were a lot, and we won."

The man lowered his head.

To Dexter I said, "Which of these six do you trust?"

"None." He started to point, "That one raped and killed; that one hung people who spoke out against them; I've seen the others hanging around with Duncan." He raised the pistol.

"No, we're not murderers," I said. He lowered the weapon and looked at me in wonder.

Tom called on the radio saying he had all the hostages. He warned us that a load of roamers were on the way. I replied and told him to get back to the hotel.

"Roger that," he agreed.

"Tie them up, and leave them to the roamers," I said. "Jess, Tony and Paul with me, the rest of you back to the cars, then back to the hotel. We'll have a debrief when we get back."

Chapter Twenty-Five

We could hear shouting coming from the house. It was a large, two story which had a field as a back yard. We travelled to it via the hostage house and the woodland so we could stay covered. We all lay on the ground, Tony and I looking through binoculars. There were no guards to see from this side, but we did see Duncan's face appear at the windows looking for his men to return with news.

"Go and look, you stupid cow!" we heard from the house. A crying woman came running out of it towards the road.

Paul went to get her and stop her from returning. We knew there were four women in there, now three, and that they would be no threat. We circled the house and decided to enter through the back door. Tony took out of a bag duct tape and cable ties. Jess opened the door, and I went first with my rifle raised.

We were in the kitchen; there were empty food tins on the table and work surfaces. At the sink was a girl who turned at the sound of the door opening. She was about to scream; I hushed her quickly, my finger to my lips. She covered her mouth with her hands. Tony went over to her and placed her in a chair, tying her hands behind her back.

Jess went to her and whispered, "If you're quiet, you live." Then she asked how many and where. The girl told us that two, plus Duncan, were upstairs. We left her there and slowly made our way up the stairs – they creaked.

"About time, bitch," said Duncan. "I'm in the back room,

can't see your dumb sister, should be on her way back by now."

Jess put on a simpering voice, "Yes, Duncan." She looked at me and shrugged her shoulders.

We picked up speed – he knew someone was coming. The end-room door was open. Just as we got to it, a naked girl walked by the opening. Turning towards us, she stopped in her tracks. We weren't who she thought we were – she screamed.

"What the fu ..." he came to the door and froze. He was standing there in shorts and a vest. He turned to the window and made a break for it. I moved quickly, dropping my rifle to my side. I ran at him, gave him a rugby tackle; we struggled for a few seconds, then I had him in a neck hold, calling to the others to tie the girls up. Within half a minute, they were bound. I lifted Duncan to his feet, still with my arms around his neck. He was starting to go red, so I eased off a little and frog marched him into another room. Paul came up the stairs and walked in on us.

"Blimey, you got the bastard!" he said smiling. "The girls are downstairs on the floor, near the other one."

"Get that chair," I said. He pulled a chair from the wall and placed it in front of us. I pushed Duncan into it, then Tony tied him up, putting duct tape over his mouth.

We stood looking at the man who led about a hundred people by fear, torture and murder. He was worse than Saddam Hussain, Hitler and Pol Pot together, all of whom murdered to gain power. We wondered what to do with him now we had him. There were no police or court systems now; it was Wild West law. We were judge, jury and executioners.

I told Jess to go and take the girls downstairs and question them. If they were loyal to this piece of muck, leave them tied, if they weren't, take them back to the hotel.

Duncan's eyes held a look of total fear; they dashed from man to man, then back. It was when Paul went up to him, put his hook up his nose and asked what was to be done that he wet himself. Tears started to roll down his cheeks, with snot coming from his nose. He was trying to say something.

Paul stood back, looked at me and said, "This piece of shit is worth nothing." His disgust had turned in to contempt. He left the room, going down to see Jess.

Duncan's eyes followed him out, and then they turned back to us. Again, he looked back and forth between Tony and me.

I walked up to him and pulled the tape from his mouth. He moaned in pain as it tore some of the stubble from his face.

"What's your story?" I said. "Why all this, and why come after me?"

He looked at me for some time, thinking. There was a puzzled look, and then he said, "You're Nick Hutchinson?"

"Eh, yes, who else would I be?" I replied sarcastically.

He looked to the door and back, "I thought you were the man with the hook."

"Why would you think that?"

"He seems a tough man, and when we've watched you he seemed to be in the lead."

"That's because he's a brave and true friend. I would give my life for him and him me."

He went into himself for a moment. He looked back at me, "Wish I had that ..."

"You had people willing to die for you, but you weren't willing to die for them. You are just a psycho with a God complex. Who are you, anyway?"

Paul came back upstairs to tell us that Jess was taking the girls to the hotel. They told her how Duncan would pick a few girls a week, call them his wives and make them do sex acts on him and his lieutenants. Then he would give them away or have them hanged.

146

"So, how did you end up with a band of thugs that would do your bidding?"

He told us his story. He was in the prison across the road from the Royal Infirmary Hospital; he was a con-man who had stolen thousands from the old and vulnerable. One day a guard took a prisoner to the hospital for a checkup and was attacked by a patient there. Within hours he was dead; he woke up and started to attack people.

It spread like wildfire through the prison; people panicked, and in the rush to escape the madness, many were crushed. The more murderous inmates killed people to get free. Duncan was in his cell and waited out the chaos, then slowly made his way to freedom. The guards had opened the doors to escape, so the passages were free of people. The dead that rose followed the living out – he met the odd one, making it past them as they were slow.

Once out of the prison, chaos reigned. Outside, there were dead everywhere. Duncan was chased, escaping into the park next door, which had a fence all around. There were others in there with him, though they were all surrounded. Luckily, the fence was solid steel and about one and a half metres high, so the dead couldn't get over.

The men inside started to panic. It was Duncan who came up with the idea to throw some of the smaller men out as bait for the dead. They screamed as some of the bigger men just picked them up and threw them over. The noise drew the dead towards them. The bait ran for their lives; some escaped, others were caught, but it was enough for the rest to get away.

Once on their travels, they found cars and other people to join them. They made their way to Groby by going up the A50. Most of the village had gone, so they set up in the community college. The kitchens were stocked; they had food. Duncan taught them how to cook on fires; he was in the Territorial Army when he was younger and knew some useful skills. At the back of the school was a wood, and in the middle was a house – that was where Duncan lived. The former prisoners became his police force, and if anybody questioned his actions they were hung from a tree.

He would send out parties of people to find more food and followers. One day they saw a car coming from the hospital. They tried to follow but lost it. Every few days he would send someone out to look for us. Then, one day, they saw smoke, and that's when they found us.

Duncan came up with a plan to capture us, as we seemed to have a very comfortable life. He never once thought we would fight back. Once we were gone, they ransacked the street and burned it down. After a while, they found the rich estate near the castle. Again, smoke gave us away, and when David stumbled onto their group, they wanted revenge. They didn't count on the guns, however.

Again we escaped, until they found us at the farm house. He said if they had been ten minutes earlier, they would have got us. So they followed us down the M1 but could not find us. When they got to London, the main road had been blocked. When they tried to work around it, there were too many dead, so they backtracked to Elstree and kept a watch on the motorway. That's when they found us again, and the rest was history.

We stood and listened to him telling his story – I couldn't believe how lucky we were. But now I had this wannabe dictator, sitting tied to a chair ... *What to do?* Paul and Tony looked at me and me at them. I drew out my pistol, turned to Duncan and shot him in the top of his leg. He started to bleed out; he would be dead in hours. I cut his ties, and we left.

Chapter Twenty-Six

We walked into the hotel dining room to cheers and hand-shakes. People crowded around us, asking about Duncan. I asked everyone to be quiet and to sit down. I told them to have something to eat and drink while I talked to my people about the attack. I needed to debrief everyone properly.

Jess and Emily had gone upstairs to Neave, while Flo made food and drinks for everyone. The rest of us went into the manager's office to talk. I told them about my part and what had happened, and then they told me theirs.

Once the order had come through to go, they started the diversion. They were surprised at how many came out so quickly. With concentrated fire, they downed a lot of defenders before they got to them. They were flanked by a few, which resulted in the hand-to-hand fighting, and only a few of ours were killed in this small skirmish. Jason and Rachael got the few that had turned, with the big gun. They could see that most of the dead had started to rise. The main battle lasted all of twenty minutes. We felt that most of the defending force may have been bullied into fighting. We were glad that any children were kept as hostages, so they weren't killed in the firefight.

After half an hour, we went back into the dining room to debrief the newcomers. I told them what had happened to Duncan and his lieutenants. We needed to know what they wanted to do: come with us, go back to Leicester or stay here. All I knew at that point was that we couldn't protect, or give weapons to anybody who went back or stayed. From what Duncan said about London, we needed everything we had. Again, the room went noisy, everyone wanting their say. I proposed to take the rest of the day off, and we would go around talking to people.

I set up a guard, as roamers were still making their way to us, but only in dribs and drabs. Rachael, Paul, Jayne and I chatted to people to get their points of view. The general feeling was that most wanted to come with us; they finally felt safe with someone to look after them.

I called a mini meeting for my people, and told them what the new survivors had said. *How would we follow through going to London with a bigger group?* I didn't mind them coming, but I didn't want freeloaders. Everyone had to have a place, a job to do. If they started to depend on us too much, accidents would happen, food would run short. I wasn't sure what to do, and neither were the others. I just couldn't leave them to die or get killed, but I simply couldn't take them all. *Should we ration the guns and food out? Should I ask my people to stay and look after them, while I take a team to London?* We were undecided, our questions and answers going around in circles. I was getting frustrated.

I went out for a walk with Rachael, Jess and Neave. I needed a break and some family time. We walked around the service area and hotel site. I wanted to see if we could fortify the area in any way. Perhaps people could stay here and look after themselves. It looked very doubtful: the area was just too big and open. It would take months to make it totally safe.

Neave loved the granddad time and she held my hand. She also kept pointing out roamers, telling me to kill them. She would giggle when they fell to the floor. *What had this world done to her?* She should have been playing with dolls and friends her own age. Now that we had new members, there were some children but not Neave's age. They ranged from eight to sixteen. They still had a look of terror on their faces from what they had experienced at the hands of Duncan.

I really didn't want to take them to a worse area. I made up my mind, and when I got back to the hotel I called yet another meeting. I didn't want to make choices for other peoples' lives; I would give them the chance to make their own minds up.

The dining room was full of chatter that went quiet when I stood up. All eyes were on me; I felt very small in front of all these people. I could see hope and faith on their faces – that was why it was so easy for Duncan to control them. These people were sheep, not wolves like Duncan and me. How these people survived at all was a mystery. They must have been in the right place at the right time; for his faults, he did keep most of them alive.

"I want to say thank you for being patient while we sorted you out. I didn't want to just leave you alone after what has happened. But I can't take all of you with me to London."

There was a lot of murmuring, some even started to cry. I held up my hands for quiet, and it worked.

"But I'm not going to leave you to fend for yourselves. I've talked to my people, and they agree that some of them will stay here with you. *But,* and it is a big *but,* you will have to do as they say. And you will all be given jobs. I'm willing to stay for a few more days to train some of you, and even help identify some people to take charge." This cheered the room up a bit.

"The first thing to do is find a more secure location. I did think about where you have just come from, in Elstree. With the noise of gunfire, though, it will have attracted roamers. It would take a lot of time to clear them out. So, from tomorrow morning, I'm sending out patrols to find somewhere else."

Again noise broke out, looking over the group, some looked worried, others excited.

"I wouldn't be sending you out unarmed. You will have a weapon and be with someone who has a gun. They will also teach you how to get around roamers without being noticed – something we learned back in Kirby Muxloe."

The murmuring rose in pitch, people chatting to each other. I started again.

"So, for now, rest and relax. My people will be on guard overnight, so it should be quiet." With that the room started to empty.

I went over to Jackson before he left and asked to see him later. I told him to give me about an hour. I then asked Tom and Flo to audit the ammunition and weapons. I arranged the guard for the night; I told them that we would all take a shift, so I sent them to bed, ready for the long night.

I next went and had something to eat. While I was deciding what to have, I asked Rose to audit the food. There and then she told me that if we didn't get more supplies soon, we would be out in two days. With the new influx of people, it would go down quickly; without them, maybe a week. So when I sent out the patrols the next day, food was on the list.

As I sat eating some stew, Jackson came in and sat opposite me. I took a swig of tea and asked him who he trusted in his group.

"To be honest, man, I only know a couple, but I'm not sure ... Some of them, they would have done anything for Duncan, but they were afraid and in awe of him. I only started to keep quiet when he threatened to hang me or hurt my kid after I asked too many questions. Look, when we attacked you, I would have killed you all for him, only because he had a hold over me. If I knew then what I know about him now, I would have taken my own chances, but it seemed safe with the group." He stopped to think; he seemed to be having some kind of inner conflict. Then he carried on, "I think they will all do as you say, they will follow anyone who is looking after them. I believe you have no worries about who to trust."

"What about leadership qualities? I need people to leave in charge – I'm leaving four of my people here to run things, but we need people to take charge when out on patrols."

He thought for a while, "There's a bloke called Darren. He nearly got hung when he asked too many questions, like me, but they beat him nearly to death instead. He did go a little withdrawn after that, not spoken to him since." He shrugged his shoulders and went quiet.

These people did have it tough; I'd find this Darren and have a word with him. Jackson sat looking at me for a few moments and me at him. "You do know I'm making you a patrol leader?" I said to him.

He was shocked, his jaw dropped, "No way, man," he said, "I've not got the balls to do that!"

"But you have," I replied. "You're a strong-minded man and you care for your people. I'll train you and Darren personally."

"But who are you Nick? How do you do all this?"

"It was thrown at me, at the start, but ask my people about me, and they will tell you the truth." I looked at him, "Because I won't." With that, I got up and took my plate and mug to be washed.

153

Chapter Twenty-Seven

The next day, I sent three groups out to find possible locations to settle. Once people woke, I changed the guard. After something to eat, those being relieved went to bed for a few hours. In each group were two of my people and two of theirs. In one group were Steve and Kelly, then there were Tony and Jayne, then Paul and Rachael. All of the groups were under strict instruction not to engage too many Roamers. They were to only attack small groups, and then only with gut suits. There was to be no shooting unless absolutely necessary. Food was also top priority, so they had to look at shops and restaurants. Before they went, we studied the maps to pinpoint likely places: Barnet, Borehamwood and Highwood Hill.

I arranged the people that were left into small pockets to guard the site. They were each within view of the next lot. I just needed these people busy until I could sort other priorities out.

Tom and Flo were in one of the downstairs rooms with the ammunition. As I entered, I looked at Tom and asked if he was alright. He looked a little grey; I wondered if he'd been taking his tablets.

"To be honest, Nick, I feel rubbish – have since last night. Didn't sleep too well, knowing our people were out there all night protecting this lot."

"I know what you mean: I'm in conflict with myself over them. They would have killed us all without mercy, but they are also innocent. They had no choice: do or die. But they would have slaughtered us, even the baby, so why should we look after them? I just want to get away from them as soon as possible. I'm not happy leaving my people with them."

"Nick, you're a good man; you're not like that madman Duncan. You are a caring and giving person – not a murderer. So Nick, you're doing the right thing: you're giving people a choice and not dictating."

"Tom, you take it easy and get some sleep if you need to. Flo, if he gets any worse, call me, alright?" They both said yes.

"Right, before I go, how's the ammo looking?"

"Not too bad yet," said Tom, "but if we have any more skirmishes, like yesterday, it won't last long. The .50 cal is looking low though, so if we could use that less it would be ideal."

I thanked them both and left. I toured the guard, making sure everything was fine. I caught a couple of people snoozing and gave them a bollocking. They said they were sorry, and that they were tired. I nearly pulled my pistol out and shot them, going a bit mad. I told them that my people had been up all night, watching out for them. Even now some of them were out there finding them a safe place to live.

I marched back to the hotel and called Jackson and Darren in. I took them to the manager's office and closed the door with a slam. Both men jumped at the sound.

"You okay, man?" asked Jackson.

"Yes," I said, rather sharply. "Are you two up to leading your group – yes or no?"

"If you think we can do it, yes," said Jackson. Darren looked at Jackson and then at me; he nodded.

"Darren, can you make the right decision in a crisis and die for the people out there?" I pointed towards the door, he nodded again.

"Well, I don't think so. You've not spoken to me or answered my questions. I don't want you here, get out!" I shouted – my temper was starting to rise. Why did I save these people? In this new world, it was survival of the fittest. Only the strong would rule the earth now. It was us or the dead, and I was not going to be ruled by them.

"I can do it," he said, his voice was strong and deep.

"Will you put yourself in front of the children in times of danger; die for the group if it comes to it?" My tone was fierce.

"I would kill for these people and die for them. I would make sure they were alive when all the others fall." His tone was just as fierce as mine.

I rested back into the chair, and said a silent 'thank you'.

"Right, from now, and for the next two days, we are leaving here and going out to kill roamers. We are going to live off the land, and I'm going to teach you how to survive. And all we are taking are knives." Their jaws dropped, then they looked at each other and back at me.

"Go, and get ready to leave in one hour. Get a good knife from Tom; I'll tell him your coming." There was quiet for a good minute; them looking at me and me at them. I broke it with a nod, and off they went.

Next I went looking for Jason but couldn't find him. A thought hit me, so I went up to Neave's room, and there he was with her, playing her favourite game – tea time at Doc Mcstuffins. Emily was sitting close to him, laughing at every word he said. He would look at her and she at him. I just hoped Jess didn't know about this new romance, but then again, she didn't want him anymore.

I knocked on the door and all three looked at me. Neave jumped, shouted "Granddad," and bounced into my arms, giving me wet kisses and hugs. I'll say it again: God I loved this girl.

"Jason, we need to talk," I said, giving Neave wet granddad's kisses, which ended with a lick on her cheek.

"Oh granddad, that's gross," and she licked me back, right from my chin, up across my nose and eyes, to my forehead. She laughed as much as I did.

"I've just got talk to daddy then he'll be back, OK sweet?"

She let go and went back to the tea party. I took Jason into the hallway, and shut the door.

"I'm off for a few days, training the new leaders. Your job is her," I said, pointing to the door. "If trouble comes, you protect her and no one else. No one goes near her. If they do, you kill them, no questions. The only people that can see her are her mother and nana, understand?" It wasn't a question but an order.

"Yes, sir," he said. "I'll do my best."

"You'll do better. If she has to die, one bullet through the back of the head. She is to feel no pain."

"I will die saving her, sir, and my last breath will be her death, sir," he was hard, I was proud of him. He was finally becoming the man I wanted for my daughter. It was a shame that it was too late for them. I shook his hand and left.

I went back to Tom and Flo and told them about Jackson and Darren, and also about Jason. Then I told them that Paul was in charge while I was gone. I said my goodbyes and went to my room to sort out my kit. I was sat on the edge of the bed thinking about the training, when Jess came in and sat next to me. I put my arm around her and gave a hug.

"You alright dad?" she asked. "You seem tense."

"I'm worried about these people, can we truly trust them? I don't want people to die, but I don't want our people to stay. I want them with us, just in case we need to fight our way out of anywhere, or in. I'd feel safer if we had them with us."

"Who are you planning to leave behind?" she asked.

"I'm thinking of asking Tony and Jayne, with Steve and

Kelly. Tony is pretty good at most things, and the others are in good minds to make decisions. But they are also good back up for me; if I need help, they seem to read my thoughts and act on them ..."

"So you wouldn't leave Jason?"

"I couldn't take him away from his kid. He loves her, and she has really bonded with him. Plus he has changed, he's better now that he has grown up and finally become a man." I wasn't going to mention Emily and what I'd seen in the room.

"Well dad, I've met a bloke. He was one of Duncan's party, and we seemed to connect. I know Emily has fallen for Jason. So why don't we stay and you take one of the others?"

Wow, I was speechless: she knew about Jason, and she's seeing another man? "Who is he?" I asked.

"His name is Charles Cooper. We fought at the battle together. We talked before and seemed to click, and he saved my life. A man was creeping up on me; Charles threw his knife and got him in the eye. I turned and killed him."

"But I want you with me. What if something goes wrong with these people; I couldn't live with myself if you and Neave died."

"Dad, you've trained me well. If there's one thing I know, it is that I'll survive and protect Neave. I'll train her, as you have me, and she'll be a survivor. She'll be stronger than us in some way: she was born into this. She'll never remember the old life, but I'll teach her about it and tell her about you."

Tears were starting in my eyes, I hugged her and didn't want to let go; my baby was all grown up. I asked her to introduce me to Charles, because I was going to take him with me to train up. If she was going to stay, then she was going to be the leader of this group, with the others as advisers. Charles would need to be able to look after my babies.

Chapter Twenty-Eight

The next two days of training were great; it took me back to my days in the forces when I was in Bosnia and Northern Ireland. We would put out OP's to watch the enemy and report movement of vehicles and personnel – we'd get into a few firefights.

This was just the same; I taught the guys how to build an OP, and how to camouflage themselves to blend into the surrounding area. We went and got a roamer and turned it into a gut suit and walked around with the dead. We set traps for rabbits and other wildlife and lived off them. Jackson and Darren were in their element, but Charles was a little unsure of some of the tactics. He was slowly picking some of it up though.

I did have to smile when I thought of poor Charles – he wasn't much older than Jess. When he saw me coming towards him with Jess, I thought he was going to run. Jess introduced him, he put his hand out but I didn't take it. I just said, "You, with me, now," and walked towards one of the cars. Jess gave me the 'dad, you bastard' smile and went back inside. I told Charles what he was going to do and why. I sent him off to pack his stuff, and I went to find Jackson and Darren.

After studying the maps, I came up with a wooded area about six miles away. On the drive there, I talked about the gut suits and how we found out about them. Yes, it was disgusting but effective. I also told them Jess's story about the shopping centre – how they walked through about a hundred of them. Charles asked why we didn't wear them all the time. I told him that the gut suit was rotting flesh, and if it got into a wound or an eye it could cause an infection or worse.

In the hours of the last afternoon, before we were to pack up and head back, we sat in the OP watching a group of roamers. I was teaching the men to write everything down, so they had an idea how to report observations. I noticed something strange about the group of affected. I picked up my binoculars to get a better look, and told the guys to do the same. What we saw were four roamers facing each other. One raised its arm in our direction, and then the others lifted their heads, as if to smell the air. Another raised its arm, but in the other direction, they all smelt the air, turned and started to walk away from us.

"Quick, follow them," I said.

We slowly climbed out of the OP and made our way around the group. We came up on a loan roamer, so I put my knife through its head, and we quickly refreshed our gut suits. It was times like this that I was glad roamers were slow walkers – we soon caught up but kept our distance and followed.

Every now and again, they stopped and sniffed the air, then they moved on. I wanted to try and circle them to get in front and see what they were up to. I told Darren and Jackson to keep following, while Charles and I went off. We were in front of the roamers, and we hid as they came close. As they passed, one stopped and looked in our direction. It tilted its head like a dog watching TV. It then turned on its way again. We were circling them when I smelled smoke.

About a hundred metres away was a camp of people. I could make out six all together: four men, two women. They had three tents; the dome-shaped ones that were quick to put up. As we moved close, I could hear them talking. I waited; there were only four roamers and six of them. They should've been able to take the dead easily when they showed up.

I heard a twig snap, and so did the campers. I turned towards the noise, and couldn't see the roamers yet. A man got up and walked towards us, then another twig snapped somewhere across from us. The man turned towards it, and shouted back that it might only be a fox. A woman came to him, and just as she moved, the roamers came out into the clearing, opposite from where we were. They took a person each. The other two ran back, drawing their weapons. The woman killed one, but two were on her quick, biting into her throat, pulling flesh and sinew from her. The other took her eye out and sucked it in like a sweet. The woman screamed in the pain as she died. The man was taken by the last one: it pushed its fingers into his eyes and then started to eat his face. His scream didn't last long, either. Then the three roamers stood up, looked at what they had done and started to walk away.

To my left, I heard movement, it was Darren and Jackson. We moved in on them and made them jump.

"Shit, you scared me, did you just see that?" said Darren.

"Bloody right I did, they coordinated their attack. They must have moved around them after they passed us, and one of the bastards even looked our way – it knew we were there."

"They never even ate them; they just murdered them and left them there," said Jackson.

"They could either smell the fire or them," I said. "I smelt it from about half a mile, and I think the wind was blowing our way. But they must have sensed it from at least two miles."

Charles had said nothing, he was just looking at the scene. I asked if he was okay – he threw up.

"Surely that's not your first roamer attack?" asked Jackson.

He shook his head and threw up again. I heard a rustle and turned to see the roamers walking back towards us. I hushed everyone, we were still in hiding. We drew our knives and waited.

They seemed to stop, look at each other and move on. They stopped again, this time a little nearer. They seemed to be scanning the area, raising their heads, sniffing the air. One pointed our way, then another did the same. They started to spread around us, but we could still see them. I pointed to each person, and then to a roamer; my men nodded. When they were just about on top of us, we jumped at them, putting them down. We stood over them, looking, trying to work out the difference between these roamers and the others. I checked their clothes and found wallets. I put them in my pocket.

Just as we stood up, I heard a moan. We turned around, and the campers that had just been murdered were standing there, looking at us. They looked at each other, sniffed the air and walked away.

"Man, that was weird!" said Jackson. "They looked at us and left!"

"We have to kill them," I said. "If they have mutated into something worse, we can't let it spread."

We carved up one of the dead ones on the floor, reapplied our gut suits, and started to follow them. It was hard to keep quiet in the wood. We finally found them, but there were only three. They were standing facing us. I quickly looked around for the others, but they were nowhere to be seen.

We charged them.

Just as we got to them, they moved to the side. We had to stop and change our direction – they started to back away. Darren was running at one when a hand grabbed his leg and pulled him down. They were lying down in the scrub, ready to ambush us.

Jackson and I backed off; I had to pull Charles back. A hand grabbed my leg. As I looked down, I saw a roamer looking up at me, so I tried to stamp on its head, my foot slipping off. The skull was still strong; it only had been killed moments before. I still had my knife in hand, so I dropped on the body, pushing the knife into its head. I had to prise its hand off. Once I was back on my feet, I looked over to my men: Darren was dead, Jackson and Charles were running for their lives. The remaining beasts were making for me, so I ran as fast as I could, soon catching up with the others.

After what seemed like a mile, I called us to a halt, "Right, back to the OP, collect our gear, and back to the hotel, we need to talk about this more."

So off we went. The roamers we had been watching were gone when we arrived back at the OP. We quickly packed and made our way to the car. Adhering to the training I had taught them, we boxed around any roamers we encountered and carried on. When we got to the road, I made everyone wait: it's standard operation procedure to wait and check the area for anything suspicious.

We gave it twenty minutes, then I sent Charles to check our ride. He walked over to it, looking around him at all times. When he got to the car he went down, checking underneath it. He stood up and gave us the all clear. We ran over to him, watching at all times – it felt a little weird, not doing it with a rifle, but we did fine. With a sigh of relief, I started the car, and we headed back with our new piece of the puzzle.

Chapter Twenty-Nine

The drive back was quiet; we were thinking about the new roamers and our lost companion. Charles was looking a little green around the gills. Jackson had his head in his hands; he would take a deep breath, sigh, shake his head and put it back into his palms. I was thinking about Darren: was he this new type of Zombie? (There, I've said it.) They ambushed us; they moved out of the way. They were *thinking*, but were they the people they were before? I just didn't know.

As I pulled into the car park, I saw people on guard, and they seemed happy as they waved us by. Pulling up in front of the hotel, Rachael came storming out – she looked like thunder. She walked straight over to me and gave me a hug.

"You bastard, you went and never said goodbye to me! You couldn't wait a few hours till I returned, just swanning off being Mr Army! And you stink!" She finally looked at my face, "What's happened?" She looked at my group, who were getting out of the car, then back at me, "Didn't four of you go?"

"I'll tell you inside, we need a drink." I motioned the two men to follow, and we went inside. Going straight to the manager's office, I sat in his chair, and told the other two to sit down. As Rachael came in, I asked her to fetch the others and a bottle of something strong.

Once everyone except Emily, Jason and Neave were in, I asked if they had found any suitable sites. They said that they found some promising places, but they needed a lot of work to secure. That wasn't reassuring, so I told people to go out tomorrow and pick the best place. At least then we could get the new people working on securing it. It would make them feel a part of their home and community. I asked Tony and Jayne to oversee the project; they needed someone with construction knowledge, and he was the man. Also, I told them that Jess and Jason were to stay and help as well, along with Emily and Neave. They would be part of the community's council, with Jackson as newbie representative. I would leave them half the ammo and guns; we would only take what we needed. The APC would stay here, and we would only take the lorry and a couple of cars. I was going to London.

Tony and Jayne looked at each other and nodded, both saying yes together.

On the plus side, they had found a superstore full of goods with little roamer activity. They went back yesterday with the lorry and extra people and filled it. There was enough food to go around, and we could take loads with us. They could fetch more from the store after they had sorted a place out, as and when they needed it.

I told them about the new threat and what had happened to us on training. How the roamers seemed to talk without talking and planned their attacks.

"Was the whole hoard like that, or just the four?" asked Paul.

"From what we saw, it was just the four. They were together and left together; the others just hung around like the normal ones," I answered.

"And the six that they, as you say ... murdered, were they the same when they turned? Why not kill you there and then, why lead you away?" asked Kelly.

"That's right; they stood and watched us kill the others, then left."

From Paul: "Fricking hell, Nick, so if they kill anyone, they themselves turn into this new beast?"

"Wished you told us first," laughed Jayne, "I wouldn't have volunteered to stay."

"That's a thought: you'll still be in this area," I said. *What would I do? I couldn't leave them there, not with the new problem. If more people turned into those things, that could mean trouble.*

"Eh, just one thing," it was Jess, "how many people have we seen since this whole thing started?" She didn't need to wait for a reply – she'd answered her own question. "Not many at all. Yes, we had the problem with Duncan, and that was a big group, but we haven't seen others." She looked around at the us. We looked at her. I looked at her. What was she getting at?

She continued, "So where is the problem? There aren't enough people to turn into uber dead. They might simply be harder to kill. We just have to be more careful when we come across them."

My God, she was right. My girl, she was going to make a great leader. I had nothing to worry about; she knew as much as I did. She was going to be okay.

"Dad, have you told us everything about these things?"

I had, and told her that.

"Which direction were they going when you left them?" asked Tony.

I did have to think about that, as I was running for my life at the time. "I know where you're coming from, mate. North, we were legging it north, then we turned west to the OP, then west again to the car, then to here, which was south. Let's hope they keep moving north and away from here."

"I think the quicker we get away from here the better," said Tony. "And we should go south, farther away. I think I know which site I want. I'm going now to check." He stood, and Jayne with him. Jess also got up and told Charles to come with them, he agreed. My God, she had him trained already – I smiled. Jackson nodded to me and left as well. He was part of the group's leadership now.

I looked at my people: we were shrinking by the day. So, who was left now? Paul and Rose, Steve and Kelly, Tom and Flo, Rachael and me: that made eight. I was going to miss both Jess and Neave, but we would be able to catch up to them at a later date. I just had to make sure I knew where they were. I made sure that they would leave clues for me to follow if they moved on.

We left the meeting and went to get some food. It was early evening, and I was shattered. It had been a long day, and all I wanted was sleep. But first I went into Neave's room, just to get my granddad fix. I'd not seen her for two days. After half an hour, I went to wash and then turned in for the night.

Chapter Thirty

The next morning, I'd got my remaining group to load the lorry and sort out a couple of cars for our push on to London. While they were doing that, I was in the manager's office talking to Tony and Jess about their new place. I wanted to know where it was and any problems they might face.

Tony showed me on the map the farm they had selected. It was called Folly Farm, and it was in the middle of nowhere. They found it by accident when they got lost on a back road. It had a barn and stables that they could convert into living compartments. The place also had gas and electric, like our old home. Tony said that the cookers were electric, so cooked food was assured. The gas was to produce hot water for the heating, but he said that once that had run dry, he might be able to convert it to electric; they had time to do that. The main problem was food itself. Once the superstore ran out, they would have to find another source, but that could wait for now. They were planning to leave the next day. He was going to get another lorry from the service yard, and they would use that to transport the food and other supplies.

By the time we had finished, the lorry and cars were packed. We hugged Jess and Neave goodbye. I didn't want to leave them; my heart was starting to break. A lump came to my throat, and tears started to form in my eyes. I looked at them both – tears were streaming down Jess' face. Rachael was crying too.

Neave just looked confused. I gave her a big, granddad kiss, and she gave me one back and said that she loved me. She said she would see me soon. I nearly broke down: I loved these girls with all of my being. I'd promised that I would always look after them, and here I was, leaving them so I could find answers that may not even be out there.

I had to find out. There might have even been a cure in Paul – weeks after the first proper bite, he was still with us and even stronger for it. How long we would be gone, I couldn't tell. The couple of days journey down had taken more than two weeks. To get to the centre of London and back could take months. We just didn't know what we were going to hit or find.

We said our goodbyes to the others. Hugs and kisses were passed around. This was family we were leaving; we hoped to be back, but we might never see them again.

Jayne and Tony finally pushed us away and told us to go. Tony joked, saying that he couldn't become a dictator with us still there. We laughed and climbed into our vehicles, driving out to cheers of good luck and waves. I was driving a BMW 5 series, Steve and Kelly were in the lorry, with Paul and the rest in a people carrier. We pulled onto the motorway and headed towards London, and, hopefully, to answers and salvation.

The lorry took the lead once we left the services. It was high up and could see farther than the rest of us. Steve and Kelly would be able see trouble before we got to it. We still had use of the radios. We had one for each vehicle, and left the rest back at the hotel. Once at the farm, they could charge them. We didn't know how long they would last; they hadn't been charged for weeks – they could go at any minute. I did leave one in the boot, just to call Jess. I told her to check after two weeks, every midday, and listen for ten minutes. If we were returning, they would know. I doubted if they would last that long, though, even the spare.

There weren't many cars on our side of the motorway, but the other was full. They were bumper to bumper, and most were empty. Some had roamers in them. I didn't see any with plain-old dead people, like we saw on the trip down. I was still a little puzzled by that phenomenon. I kept a look out for them; if I saw any, I wanted to check them out. Like before, we would stop to check ahead, but activity was very minimal. We would see the odd roamer wandering around, but we just drove straight by.

We came to the end of the motorway and turned right, as we wanted to go down Edgware Road. It was fenced off, so we travelled further round the North Circular. It was the same at every junction. After about two miles, we saw that the dead were starting to grow in number. We stopped at Brent River, stood on the roof of the lorry and saw thousands of them, just standing there at the fences. If they pushed, I was sure they would put over the fences, but they just waited there. It was just like Duncan had said; was it like this all round the city? I wasn't going to find out.

We turned around and headed back to Edgware Road. We brought tools with us that could undo the fences – we would pass through. It only took Paul and me minutes to open one, let the vehicles through and close it again. Just as we tightened the last nut, a roamer wandered up from the right. We watched it come up to the fence and reach through, growling and moaning at us. I went up to it and put my knife up through its chin, killing it.

This side of the fence was like a ghost town: there were no bodies anywhere, not even signs of damage. Had the city been evacuated when the trouble started? There was nothing on the news before the blackout, but this could have happened after then. Maybe they still had local news once the national closed down.

We drove down Edgware road; it changed back to the A5 after a while. There were no vehicles in the middle of the road; they were all parked up nicely at the curbs. It all felt very weird.

We carried on through Cricklewood Broadway. Down the Kilburn High Road, the silence was scary. Only birds were moving about on the rooftops, and they seemed to be watching us. I did get an eerie feeling, like we were being watched, but I put that down to the birds. Maida Vale and the other Edgware Road were just the same – quiet and still. It took us nearly an hour to travel this far. We didn't want to rush and get ourselves trapped or worse.

When we got to Marble Arch, we stopped and got out to have a break and something to eat. We sat on the benches just past the arch, each lost in our own thoughts.

"It's too fricking quiet," said Paul, "where is everyone? No fricking morons trying to kill us, and the dead: there should be at least a couple, but I've not seen one since we got in."

"What happened here?" said Kelly.

It was Tom who voiced my earlier thought about an evacuation, and we all agreed on that.

"But surely someone must still be around?" said Steve, "There are no bodies. It's too clean – someone must have got rid of them."

We'd been going round like this for ages, when Flo told us all to be quiet and listen. We all stopped talking. There was a soft thudding and humming. Everyone started looking around for the source; I was the only one looking skyward. There it was: a Chinook helicopter coming up from the south. I pointed to it, and they all turned to see the helicopter flying towards us. We jumped up and started to shout and wave. It circled us a few times; I could see the pilot looking at us as he passed. It started to land on the road, just down from us. We waited to see what was going to happen.

As it landed, a platoon of men deployed from the back, all dressed in black and gas masks. I told everyone to take off their pistols and put them on the ground. Within seconds, we were surrounded and had rifles pointing at us. I tried to see if there were any regimental badges, so I could identify them, but there were none. I walked forward and told them my name and where we had come from. From the back a voice said that he was coming through.

A large man, dressed the same as the others, walked through the line. On his shoulders were the three pips of a captain. I still don't know why I did it, but I saluted him. I smiled as he returned my salute.

"Your name sounds familiar," he said.

"I was in 22 Regiment, sir," I replied.

"And which squadron were you in?"

"C Squadron, sir."

"Hutchinson ... Hutchinson ..." he pondered. "Hutch! That's what the lads called you, RSM Hutchinson, I remember you," he took his mask off; I knew the face but couldn't place the name.

"You don't remember me ... I was a new Rupert, and you bollocked me for making men salute. You told me that in the regiment, we didn't salute a Rupert until they'd done time in there and been on a couple of jobs."

Oh yes, I remembered him: Culverwell – turned out quite good, if I remembered properly. Went into Afghanistan and did three tours, back-to-back. The blokes loved him after that.

"Yes, sir, hope you won't hold it against me now, sir," I smiled; he smiled back.

172

"You made me the man I am today. I wouldn't be here if it wasn't for you. After the bollocking, the men started to treat me right and made sure I was taught everything. I made captain just before the shit hit the fan. I was in Cobra just as the outbreak happened." He paused and told his men to lower their weapons.

"Why have you come here, Nick?"

"I want answers ... to a lot of questions, and hopefully the cure."

"Right, come with us, and I will take you to the prime minister."

I went to pick up my pistol, all the weapons were raised, "Sorry, Nick, you can't bring weapons in with you," he paused. "Maybe later."

We were led into the back of the Chinook, and it took off heading south.

Chapter Thirty-One

As we flew over Buckingham Palace, I saw the once well-kept grounds all overgrown. We skimmed the rooftop, and from that height the grass looked about half a metre tall; weeds grew on the paths. As we flew over the palace itself, the Royal Standard was flying. I looked over to Culverwell, and he shook his head, I nodded and mouthed 'OK'. We then flew over The Mall, again full of weeds. We passed the Horse Guards Parade, and then over the river. That's when the scene changed.

Straight away I saw the bridge next to the Embankment was gone, as were Waterloo and Blackfriars. I also could see fencing on the far bank of the river. There, to my horror, were thousands and thousands of dead just standing there, watching us fly over them.

We flew down the Thames, and the scene was the same: all the bridges were down, and there was fencing on the banks. The dead seemed never ending. I could tell that there must have been a bombing raid at some point. Most of the buildings were just rubble. Tower Bridge had lost one of it towers. The other, on our side, stood alone without its sister. Part of the over-walk was reaching out, as if to save them, but just couldn't get there. At the Tower of London, I saw soldiers. They looked up at the Chinook and carried on with their work.

The Chinook turned south over the dead. It seemed to slow down slightly, and hovered even lower. It flew like this for a couple of miles, and then went east for a few more. Eventually, the big helicopter swung back to the Thames, flew over into Purfleet, then on to Dagenham. Once back over the city we came in to land at the airport.

The Chinook set down pretty quickly; the engines shut off almost as the wheels touched the ground. The place was a hive of activity over our arrival; we were escorted off the helicopter and rushed into the airport lounge. No one said anything to us, except for directing us which way to go. Culverwell showed us into the first-class area. There, waiting, was a face I'd thought I'd never see in person. In his hand was a glass of beer, and as we walked into the room he took a sip.

"Welcome to London, I'm Prime Minister Windsor," said Prince Harry with a smile on his face. He told us to take a seat, which the others did, except for me.

Culverwell went up to him and asked if he could stay.

"Are they dangerous?" he said patting his sidearm.

"I don't know, sir," he replied.

"Alright, but you said over the radio that you knew one of them."

This was starting to piss me off: they were talking as if we weren't there.

"Yes sir, only by reputation."

"Right, but I'll do the talking."

"Yes sir."

With that, Prince Harry sat down. He took out his pistol and put it on his lap.

Looking at me, he asked who we were, and how we came to London.

"Sir, as you know, I'm Nick Hutchinson; this is my wife Rachael." I said, pointing to her. "The man with the nasty-looking hook is Paul Lancaster and his wife, Rose. This is Kelly and Steve Holley, and last of all, this is Tom and Flo

Barrow," he nodded to each person and said hello.

I went into the story from the beginning: from how we heard about the virus to being attacked, the castle, getting the guns, finding out about Duncan and fighting his army, to this moment. It took me a good two-hours of talking. I had sat down by then. We were offered drinks and food which we took.

The prime minister was quiet for some time, thinking over what I had just told him.

"Captain Culverwell tells me that your background is S.A.S."

"Yes, sir."

"Is that why you think you survived for so long?" he asked.

"I believe, sir, that my training helped, but the backup of a good team also contributed to it, sir. If I didn't have such a good team we'd all be dead by now, or even worse, one of them."

"Other than this Duncan fellow, have you had to kill other people?"

"No, sir, and we only had to kill them to survive ourselves. It was them or us."

"These uber zombies, as you call them, have you seen or encountered any more?"

"No, sir, only the ones in the wood."

"Right, do you think that there could be more of them? Would you be able to find the ones you killed?"

"To find them ... yes, I could. Given a good map, I could take you straight to them. But are there any more? I don't know about. Like I said earlier, they seem to transmit to the living, but I've never seen a roamer attack another, sir."

"That's fine, I want Mr Lancaster here to see our doctors to see if a cure can be found in his blood. Firstly, I want you all to rest until tomorrow. It's getting late now. I think some beds have been sorted for you. Tomorrow, we will assign duties, everyone has to work here for their keep."

"Thank you, sir, but I would like to know what happened to the world and how it all started."

"Mr Hutchinson, the world is dead. I'll see you all tomorrow, and if I have time, I'll tell you what I can."

The prince turned and left the room, with Culverwell following. As they left, two soldiers came in and said we were to follow.

We were taken to a local bed and breakfast. The rooms were comfortable and clean. The lights worked; there seemed to be a source of electricity. I went to the wash room and turned on a tap, water came running out. I even tried the hot-water tap, silently hoping, and there it was: hot running water. I went back into the room and told Rachael who whooped with joy and started to run the shower. The others had been taken to their own rooms. The only downside was that they were locked from the outside, so we couldn't leave. The escort had said that we would be fetched for breakfast.

We were gathered early next morning and taken down to the dining room. Breakfast was a buffet system of bacon, sausages, toast, eggs or cereals. I was amazed at the food; where did they get it from? Maybe later we would find out. We all sat at the same table and chatted among ourselves. Others in the room were watching us with a steely stare, not trusting the newcomers. We felt very vulnerable in our new surroundings, but we had to trust these people. After all, weren't they the good guys.

Chapter Thirty-Two

We had just finished our drinks when we were called out – so off we went. We were ushered to a medical centre, where we had our blood taken. Then we each were given a medical by a nurse. She was very thorough: I'd not had one like that since I joined up.

As we waited for each other to have their turn, we talked about our situation some more. We talked about the food and hot water and about what jobs we would get. We also chatted about Prince Harry who was running the show. He was a good commander back in the day when he was in Afghanistan. He stood beside his men and fought just as hard as them. He worked hard and he played hard, which always seemed to get him in trouble. I knew Joe Public didn't care, as Harry, even though he was a prince, was one of them.

I also said that I'd like to get Jess and Neave back to us. It seemed to me that people were needed here, even if it was just to make the beds and clean up.

After we had all been done, we had to wait to be collected by another escort to go and see the prime minister. We were, to our surprise, taken to 10 Downing Street. It was the obvious choice for a good base of operations – it had everything from bunkers to walls, and fenced-off gardens and streets.

We were made to wait in a small conference room. We sat around the table just looking at each other for a while. After about fifteen minutes, the door opened and Harry came in, with an aide just behind him. He said hello to everyone and apologised for all the trouble we were going through – they had to make sure we were safe and healthy.

Harry looked at Paul, turned to the aide, and asked why he was still there – Paul should have been at the hospital, having tests. The aide apologised and asked Paul to follow. Paul asked if Rose could go with him. He was told, sorry, no, as he was being taken to a secure area. Paul gave the PM a look that could kill, but followed without argument.

The PM sat at the head of the table and put a thick file in front of him. He opened the cover and looked at the first page.

"I'm sorry to say that I've had a word with the others, and they have decided that I cannot tell you what has happened or what is going on."

A knock at the door, then it opened: it was the aide again. He asked if he could have a word. The PM agreed, turned to us, and said he would be back soon. He looked me in the eye, winked and left the room.

The door shut, and I jumped up, running around the table to the file.

"Nick, should you be doing that?" asked Tom.

"He said that *he couldn't* tell us. But he said nothing about leaving the file here and us finding out for ourselves. It's an old army trick."

I sat in his seat and read the report aloud.

Basically, a clever scientist found a retrovirus that could cure cancer, even in those very close to death. The problem was with the testing: it wouldn't work on animals. That part of the trials simply wasn't possible. They used living tissue from people, and the virus attacked the cancer, reanimating the dead cells.

They needed living subjects to test further, so they went to a small country in West Africa and located people with cancer.

They paid them to take the retrovirus. It worked: the people came back healthier and better. It was a success, they had cured cancer. They would never get rid of the disease itself, but they had a cure for the condition.

The powers that be kept it quiet – they wanted to make sure there were no relapses. After a year, some of the test patients started to die. When autopsies were preformed, nothing could be found to indicate why the subjects perished. The only clue they had was the presentation of flu-like symptoms prior to death – all died within a day or two of the onset.

A few weeks after the patients started to die, one of the bodies moved. The doctors and nurses couldn't believe what was happening. The subject should not be moving: its organs had been removed. It rose from the table, moaning and hissing. It lunged for one of the nurses, taking a bite from her arm. She was taken to have the wound treated but died from what they called an infection. The only difference in the reanimated patient was that the brain had not been removed during autopsy. This wasn't realised until well after the infection spread. The nurse came back within hours of dying. She also bit people, and that's when it went wild.

It was found out later that the retrovirus mutated when people died. It was too late by this point though; it was already impossible to stop. They managed to keep it confined to Africa until a man called John Pickering, who worked on the site, couldn't handle the death and mayhem anymore, so he left. He had been scratched without realising it.

Travelling with many other passengers on a plane and boat, Pickering spread the virus unwittingly – it had become airborne, the virus taking effect only when the person died. Transmission by bites and scratches would still kill and reanimate the dead, but the new form of infection compounded the situation – everyone had the virus in their system in no time.

It wasn't realised till later that the brain had to be killed for the body to stop moving. No one understood why this was. The best theory was that the brain's electricity was the catalyst the virus needed to waken the body. Once this was stopped, the virus couldn't work on the rebuilding.

When it arrived in Britain, John Pickering died in a park at Dover. He bit a park keeper and other tourists. Some were taken to different hospitals around the country where there were secure units, but these didn't hold the rising dead. It started to spread, getting out of hand.

The airborne virus travelled far and wide, infecting everybody from the new-born babes to the nearly dead. And once that person did die, they would rise and bite or scratch anyone who came close.

All the waking dead wanted to do was eat flesh, as if an inborn, animal instinct came to the fore. When there was no stimulus, they would stand around, dormant, until someone or something came into view. Noise attracted them, and when the noise was loud, it would send them into an uncontrollable frenzy.

They had tried various ways of destroying them. Flamethrowers were used, which were only effective when the body was truly cooked. Even if part of the brain survived, the monsters would still move. They even tried bombing vast areas, but it had the same effect as the fire. They tried numerous gasses – only one killed them outright. It was tested on the M1 motorway, (which answered one of my questions). It was a nerve toxin that attacked the brain and killed it, but it was impossible to manufacture more. They were still looking for ways to kill them. In the end, the best method was to do what we had been doing from the start: bullet or knife.

Written in black pen, at the end of the report, was the summary of a new threat of the dead – a type that could think for themselves. This new breed was found near Elstree.

And then, scrawled in red: *So, in conclusion, we're fucked.*

I looked up from the report and looked at my friends. Rachael was weeping; the others had tears in their eyes too.

All I could say was, "Shit."

Chapter Thirty-Three

Over the next few weeks, we were put to task. I never saw Paul; Rose had been taken to him, but I never saw her either. When I asked about them, I was told: "He's having tests, and she's with him."

I only saw the others now and again; we never got a chance to talk, as we were never left alone. We were split up and moved to different boarding houses. Rachael was put on to general duties, and I was made part of a military training group. I helped train the inexperienced and any new people. This was the only time I had the use of a weapon. Other than that, I was never given one, even when I noticed that everyone else had a sidearm and knife.

I was also quizzed about our time after the outbreak; they seemed to ask the same questions over and over again. Even though I felt safe there, I also felt very uncomfortable. I did trust these people to make the right judgments, but why were we kept apart? I was worried about Tom and Flo. They were old, so were they of any use to them? I knew that Flo could cook and Tom could drive. Other than that, they weren't of much use. They worked well in our group, as every little helped. Here: there were more than enough healthy people to do jobs.

I did find out about how they sent patrols out to fetch food and find people. One day, whilst I was with Culverwell, I asked if we could fetch Jess and the gang. I was worried that Jess was waiting for us on the radio every day, and I didn't even have one. Did she think were dead or alive? I just didn't know.

"At the moment, we haven't the resources to cope with the amount we already have. More people would be a burden," he told me.

"I've seen you bring people in all the time: you brought us in, and we're working alright. Jess and the others are battle experienced – they could be useful."

"The only people we bring in are the ones found within the perimeter. We bring them in because we don't want them followed or turning into the infected."

"But surely we could take a helicopter and fetch them. Wouldn't you want to do the same?"

"No, I wouldn't and didn't. My family are all dead. I know that, and wouldn't waste people and fuel trying to find out."

"But I know they are alive, they can look after themselves, they just need to be brought here," I argued.

"Sorry, but *no* means *no*. This is something we agreed on when the outbreak happened. We've managed to make this part of the city safe."

I was quiet, how could I argue when the man never even went to look for his family? Once more, I persisted, "Look, Fabian, if you had the chance, would you go and try to find them? It's my only daughter and granddaughter out there. I just want them near me to make sure they are safe."

It was his turn to say nothing; I could tell he was thinking about it. He turned and looked out of the window. Once he turned back, he said, "Leave it with me," and left the room. It was a start.

Autumn was coming: the leaves on the trees were starting to change colour, and I had to start wearing a jacket at the training ground in the Queen Elizabeth Olympic Park. We had to kill roamers on a daily basis; this part of the city wasn't secure, but it helped with the training.

One day, the PM came to the training ground, just as we were killing some roamers. He walked up, pulled out his knife and helped us kill twenty or more of the beasts. Once this was done, and we were covered in sweat and blood, he called me over to have a private word.

"Captain Culverwell tells me you want to fetch your daughter and the others, is that right?"

"Yes sir," I replied.

"We have been thinking about your request and have decided to offer you a deal."

I thought: *what could I give for the life of my daughter and granddaughter?* It would be anything he asked.

"Anything, sir, I would do anything to get my family back together," I said.

"Alright then, when you've finished here, report to me at Downing Street, and I'll tell you what we need."

"Yes sir!" I said with a salute.

With that, he about turned and left the training ground. I was planning an escape and evasion exercise, but changed my mind and did a quick target practice with sniper rifles. Because of the limited supply of ammo, it wouldn't take long.

I sat in his office, waiting; I felt refreshed after a shower, cleaning away the blood and sweat. I'd grabbed a bite to eat before driving over to Downing Street with Culverwell.

In came Harry looking very tired and a little unkempt. I wondered what he'd been up to in the last few hours.

"Thanks for coming, Nick. It's been a mad day – we had a breakthrough over by the river. We lost quite a few men, but we've got the fence up now, and order has been restored." He pressed his intercom and asked for some early evening tea.

The door opened, and in walked Kelly. We did double takes as we looked at each other, smiling. She had landed a good job. She handed the PM a can of beer and asked what we would like. I asked for the same, and Culverwell asked for a diet coke. She left, and within seconds was back with the drinks. As she handed me mine, I asked if she and Steve were ok. She went red and nodded, then she left. As she was leaving, I noticed that she was wearing a sidearm, lucky her.

"Kelly was one of your group?" He asked.

"Yes, she and her husband were great right-hand men; they were probably the best on my team."

"Yes, I got that impression when I interviewed them; Stephen is part of my security team."

"What about the others? Is Tom alright? He's not a well man, and Paul ... I've not seen him or Rose since the first day."

"Oh, right," he looked a little embarrassed, "Tom died three weeks ago of a heart attack."

My blood was starting to boil: no one had the bottle to tell me? *Bastards.* I told myself to cool it. I needed to get Jess and Neave back, and going ballistic at the prime minister was not the thing to do.

"What happened to his body?"

"The brain was decommissioned and the body burnt. That's what we do with our dead. There is no time to keep digging graves; we just burn them with dignity."

The room fell into silence. I said a private goodbye to Tom; but what of Flo? Where was she, and was she alright? And nothing was said about Paul.

"To business, the deal I have for you is this: our boffins want an uber zombie, alive if possible. We want to know how clever they really are. The normal ones are easy to understand:

all they want to do is eat you, noise distracts them. But from your report, the ubers killed these people and left them. When the dead turned, they lured you into a trap."

I nodded in agreement. "Sir, do you want me to go and find an uber and capture it, while you get my girls and the rest of the group?"

"Well, yes and no: you'll be part of the team that goes. You'll take them to where you found the ubers. Once the beast is back here, and we're happy with it, then your people will be collected."

I wasn't happy with this; I would be risking my life and still wouldn't have my girls back. I tried to negotiate a better deal: I would go in with the team once the uber was caught. I would go and fetch the others, and we would make our way back.

"I can't give you any men, it will just be you on your own," he said, after some thought.

"Can I at least have the people I came with: Kelly, Steve, Rachael and Paul?" I countered.

"Sorry, no, I need everyone here. The infected are getting more restless; I need everyone to man the fences."

"A least give me Paul. He's stuck in the hospital; he would love to get out and do some work."

"Nick, he is a very important person at the moment. We believe there will be a breakthrough very soon. Once an antivirus vaccine has been developed, he can leave and become part of the team."

I had to give up; at least I could go on my own. I would make sure they tooled me up with plenty of ammunition and firepower. I told him this, and also told him that from now on, I wanted my own sidearm. Everyone else had one but Rachael and me. Again, he mulled it over; eventually he agreed. I then told him that I would need the radio out of the car we came in, so I could contact Jess when I got close. He told me that all of our gear was in storage, and the radio would be collected.

At last, I was getting somewhere.

"When do we go?" I asked.

"In two days. We have to prep the vehicles, then get a plan of action finalized. We'll be meeting back here in two days at 0900 hours," he was finished.

I got up and left his office. It was starting to get dark, so I went back to my digs and had dinner with Rachael. I told her about my day.

"So, why can't I go? All I do all day is clean these rooms and fetch the food from stores. I feel like a spare part around here, and why does everyone but us have a weapon?" She was starting rant about being here, about how she felt not trusted and kept in the dark about everything.

I told her how I felt the same; like when I found out about Kelly and Steve. That's when I remembered about Tom and told her. Rachael burst into tears and asked about Flo. All I could tell her is what the PM told me.

We talked into the night and tried to work out a plan to get her to come with me on the mission.

Chapter Thirty-Four

Early next morning, I sat in Culverwell's office with two lieutenants and two sergeants. We were talking about the mission
and how we would capture the uber. One idea was to shoot
the kneecaps so it couldn't walk, then put a hessian bag over
its head to stop it from biting. It turned out to be a bad idea: it
would mean carrying it.

Others were thrown about, but the best idea we came up with
was to use a ketch pole: it's a noose on the end of a pole. You
put the noose over the head and pull it tight. The beast would be
out of arm's reach, and you could push or pull it to where you
wanted. We would still use a hessian bag to cover the head; we
would also cable tie the hands. If these things were as clever as
we thought, they might know that even a scratch would infect
and kill you, turning you into one of them.

Lots of other planning was done. We planned RVs and ERVs
just in case things went tits up. I wasn't listening as intently as
I should have been. I was making my own plans. Once we had
got the uber, I had to get to Jess and Neave. Also, I was waiting
for the right moment to get Rachael on my team, so at least I
would have a partner.

"So, Nick, anything else to add?" The voice only just broke
through my thoughts; it was Culverwell talking. I must have
had a blank look on my face as he asked the question again.

"Sorry, yes, I would still like to take Rachael with me; I need
an extra pair of eyes for map reading whilst I'm driving and

searching for the other group. I have a rough idea where they are, but I would still need the map." I said matter-of-factly.

"I talked to the PM last night, and he said if you were to ask, then yes, but only your wife – no one else," he said with a smile at the corner of his mouth.

"Thank you, sir," I said and thought: *at last, cooperation.*

Culverwell asked me to wait once the briefing was over. Once everyone had left, he went over to the cupboard and took out two pistols and knives. They were the weapons we came in with and had not seen since that first day. I had to think: nearly two months ago. He passed them over, and said that I was to report to the armoury at 1800 to collect my other weapons.

I thanked him again and said how grateful I was for letting Rachael participate in the mission.

He asked me to sit down and have afternoon tea with him, which was now the fashionable thing to say when you wanted a beer. It was a rule: you were never allowed to drink on duty. The times had changed somewhat – *just don't get drunk*, was now the main stipulation.

Over the next hour, we chatted about the old days and the regiment. He had a lot of stories as did I. I felt he needed someone to relate to; it was hard in a time like this to make friends, especially when you were in a position of authority. With me, I was somebody he knew, or even respected, and had something in common.

I checked the time: I had to go and get my stuff from the armoury. We said our goodbyes, and that we would see each other tomorrow at Downing Street.

The armoury was at the Horse Guards Barracks. Rachael and I were each given a nice semi-automatic rifle – they had built-in grenade launchers under the main barrel. We were supplied with two boxes of ammunition for each of the rifles and pistols.

I asked if there were any .50 cal rounds, thinking of the APC that was with Jess. There was none; the quartermaster told me it was like rocking horse shit. Feeling well tooled-up, I headed back to the digs for dinner to tell Rachael the good news.

Nine o'clock outside 10 Downing Street was a hive of activity: two four-ton lorries with fifteen men in each; two command Land Rovers; another smaller Land Rover modified to contain the uber; and then Rachael and me with a Range Rover. Everyone was doing something, whether it was checking weapons or the vehicles. Not a soul was still until the doors of Number 10 opened. There was a hushed command, then everyone stopped what they were doing and looked at the PM.

He was dressed as we were: all in black, face covered in camouflage cream and a big grin.

"Right men, everyone knows what we are doing and why. We need to get one of these infected and work out why they are what they are. We will bring it back alive; you know what I mean." He was returning the smiles he saw among the faces.

"I'm hoping we all come back alive ourselves, but there could be casualties. If there are, then the brain will be deactivated." Smiles were now gone; people nodded.

"We've got twenty minutes to get to the barrier, then the diversion will start, so let's get on board and move out." Everyone ran to their transport and climbed in, engines revved into life and we pulled out.

At the front was the first command Rover, then us. The uber vehicle was next, then the two lorries and, finally, the last Land Rover. We kept close quarters and travelled to the barrier at the top of the Edgeware Road. As it came into sight, we stopped and waited. Within seconds, over to the west of us at the Wembley Stadium, explosions went off, as did fireworks and what sounded like gunfire. The few dead that were hanging around turned and went off in the direction of the noise. We gave it a few minutes then opened the barrier, drove through and then closed it again.

It was my turn to take the lead and drive to where we found the uber. It was slow going on the motorway; the big lorries had to take it easy around the cars. It was a good thing that I suggested we travel along the south-bound side. I knew the north bound was full of cars and we would never have moved.

It took us two hours to travel to the service area. Like on the way down, we would periodically stop and check the road ahead. There seemed more roamers about and we had to kill them to make our way.

On arriving at the services, we were hoping to have a break and finalise the next step, but it was crawling with dead. I made a quick trip to the command vehicle, and we headed off to the uber site.

Half an hour later, we pulled up to the site where we had parked our car on the training trip. As soon as we stopped, the men in the first lorry jumped out and did an all-round defence, covering the road and woods around us. The rest climbed out, stood at the side of the road and waited. The two lieutenants and two sergeants, along with Culverwell and the PM, joined the men and then discussed the next move.

I was taking the lead again, moving through the trees with caution; I formed the tip of an arrow, the men behind me spread out to about twenty metres. Culverwell, with a group, was left back at the road. They would be our back up should we need it, and they would make sure the road and our transports remained secure.

The journey was slow, and every now and again you would hear, "Got one," as the men came across an infected and killed it.

I came to the OP that I had built and gave the signal for everyone to stop. With this, all the men went down on one knee. Each man faced a specific direction to provide all-round cover.

The PM and the lieutenant with the sergeant walked up to me and asked for a sitrep of the site. It was all clear, and I told them what happened and where. Then I moved us off towards the camp.

Rachael was to my left; she moved in closer to me. I glanced at her – she had a worried look on her face.

"You okay?" I asked in whisper.

"No, don't you feel it? Something isn't right ..." she returned, also in a whisper.

I looked up and around me, then I did feel it. The birds weren't singing, there was no noise from the undergrowth, it was still – even the air was quiet. I brought everyone to a halt; I went down on one knee, looking around. The PM shuffled up, knelt beside me and asked what was wrong.

"Sir, don't you feel it? There's nothing moving; it's as if the woods are waiting for something to happen." We knelt in silence, reaching out with our sixth sense; it talks to you when you are in danger – you learn to trust it.

"Yes, Nick, I can," his face became hard, his eyes were darting over every little thing, and I could tell his ears were pricked, listening for any little sound.

"How far is it to the camp now?"

"Not far sir, a couple of hundred metres that way."

"Okay, move off."

So I did.

Chapter Thirty-Five

The camp was cleared. No tents, no bodies and no sign of a campfire. Even after all this time, there should have been signs of what happened here. The men were in an all-round defensive position.

"Are you sure this is the place?" asked the lieutenant.

"Yes, I am, this was the site. Over there were the tents; that's where the people got attacked, and that's where we were hiding. That's where we killed the original ubers, and that is the way the new ones went. We ran off in that direction," my voice was starting to rise. Rachael squeezed my arm; I took a deep breath.

Then we heard a scream. Someone fired a gun, and all hell broke loose. The PM, lieutenant, sergeant, Rachael and I were in the middle of the unit. Our troops were firing all around us. We raised our guns, looking for the targets – and then we saw them ...

We were surrounded by roamers. The men were moving back, into the clearing, firing as they went. There must have been hundreds of them; as one went down, another would take its place.

A man tripped back and the beast was on him. He was fighting for his life, holding the beast at arm's length – it was biting at his hands and body. I took aim and shot it through the head. The man pushed it off and jumped up, shooting others that came for him.

Thankfully, we were wearing light chainmail under our cloths, and we had hard leather gloves. It was the face that wasn't protected; we had our respirators on us, but we weren't going to put them on until we knew we were going to fight. I quickly put mine on and told Rachael to do the same. I shouted the order to put them on ASAP.

I saw two men go down under a crowd of them; they got ripped apart, at least two dead on each limb. Arms and legs were just thrown aside. I was firing into the crowd but my aim was out, I was starting to panic. Every which way I turned there were dead. Men were starting to fall, fighting as they did; some were still firing, taking roamers with them. I tried to count how many were left, but I couldn't.

I saw the lieutenant go down; where was the PM? I started to look for him. I saw Rachael – she was the only woman, but I almost couldn't tell with all her gear on. I tried to make my way to her: if we were going to die, I wanted to be with her. Four roamers were making a lunge for her, and I took them out. She spun round and saw me. I quickly lifted my mask and put it back; she went back to firing.

I was on my fifth mag. I had started with twelve, so I was down to seven. I made it to Rachael and put my back to hers – we kept shooting anything that moved. Others had started to do the same, it was called watching each other's back.

I noticed that the monsters were now ducking and trying to dodge the bullets. How on earth had there gotten so many? They were still slow, so we could take them out. One of the beasts picked up a dead body and used it as a shield, but it was too heavy – it had to drop it. I shot it through the eye.

To my right, I saw roamers take down two more men. The beasts pulled the masks from their faces and bit into them, skin and eyes pulled from their skulls. I didn't hear the screams over the noise, I just fired into the melee.

To my left, another pack attacked the men. One of the monsters pulled the rifle from a soldier's hand and tossed it aside. The man's hood was pulled down and the roamer took a chunk out of his head. I took out the man and the monster – it was a mercy.

Two more mags gone, I tried again to count how many were left. I knew there weren't many, but I had other problems – roamers were getting nearer. Behind me, I heard Rachael shouting that she was out of mags. I pointed to my pouch. She took the two in there. Down to three, I thought – it was getting scary. Either side of me, my men closed in. We sustained an all-round defence, but for how long?

The man to my left shouted, asking who I was. I told him, he was the PM. The man to my right did the same, and again, I told him. He shouted thanks for saving his life. It was the man who was on the ground fighting off the roamer.

I was on my last mag; the others were down to sidearms. We only had a couple of mags for those. Running empty, I was down to my pistol as well. All I could do was aim shoot, aim shoot.

One by one, the others ran dry. I was just waiting for the end, but we still kept on fighting. I fired my last round into the head of the nearest one, then took out my knife, stabbing the closest monster, then the one after that.

It was hard going, my body was really starting to lose its strength, and I was feeling weaker by the minute. My muscles were finding it harder to wield the knife. We couldn't move with all the dead at our feet. One of the bastards got to me and pulled me down. I was under it, and I felt weight being added as more climbed on top. I lost my knife. I rolled into ball, keeping the mask to my face and my arms tight so they wouldn't pull me apart. I could feel their bites; the chain mail was doing its job.

The biting stopped – a large explosion deafened me. The pressure of the bodies was gone, then another explosion. I stayed in a ball; I wasn't going to let them get me, I was going to hold out for as long as possible. I heard shouting through the ringing in my ears. I opened my eyes, and there was the most beautiful sight anyone could wish for.

It was Jess – she was smiling at me.

"Come on, old man, we need to move before they regroup," she said, pulling me to my feet and hugging me.

I looked around: Rachael came in for a hug. There were about twelve people, all dressed in military fatigues, looking at Harry, who lifted his mask off his face. The newcomers were amazed at who was in front of them. I couldn't see my other soldier anywhere.

We started to head back to the transport when Jess told us we had to go another way. I told her that we had men back there. She said that they were all dead. I followed her with Rachael by my side and the PM just behind.

"Who's that girl?" he asked.

"My daughter," I said with pride in my voice.

"Our daughter," added Rachael.

"She's good, she is defo coming back," he said with a smile on his face.

I suddenly realised I had no weapon and asked Jess if she had a spare.

"Don't worry, Pops, we're covered," she pointed up.

I looked up, all I could see were trees. Looking back at her in puzzlement, she just laughed and said she'd tell us later. With that, we picked up our pace and made it back to her transport. There was our old, faithful APC, with Jason at the gun. Next to that were a people carrier and a fricking tank. Both the PM and I stopped in our tracks.

He looked at Jess, "You have a fucking tank!"

"Oh, and more, sir. Quick, into the APC, we are going back home," she said, smirking.

"And where's home?" he asked.

Chapter Thirty-Six

Just as we pulled into RAF Northolt, I saw a drone coming in to land. I turned to the PM and he at me.

"Did you know about this place?" I asked him.

"Yes, it was a refugee camp for the evacuees of London," he replied. "But we had no reply from them after the outbreak and assumed they had fallen." He was looking out the tiny windows, trying to get a better look around. "We've had people on the radios 24/7 trying to reach the outside ..." he trailed off.

We soon pulled up outside a building where we were greeted by the base commander. He showed us into the officers' mess. Everyone else seemed to disappear, except Jess, who walked between Rachael and me, holding our hands. I have not done that since she was a kid.

The commander turned and saw Jess and asked her to leave. All three of us declined verbally – she stayed. He went red and showed us to a couple of tables, asking us to sit down while he ordered tea and coffee.

"Your Majesty, why were you up at that site? It's a no-go area." He said like he was talking to a naughty child.

His tone seemed to upset the PM: "Before we start, what is your name, why are you still here, and why didn't you reply to our radio?" There was a roughness to his voice, "Also, I'm not royalty anymore, I'm the prime minister."

"So sorry, sir, I think I'm just used to being the top dog, so to speak. I totally forgot myself. Sir, welcome to RAF Northolt.

I'm Captain Smith of the Royal Auxiliary Corps," he stood to attention and saluted.

"You're a part-time captain?" asked the PM; he was quite angry with this man. I didn't know why. "Right, Captain Smith, my friends and I have had a hard day. We have lost a lot of good men to them things out there. I would like a shower and food, then you can tell me everything."

The captain asked Jess to show us to the accommodation block and sort out food. She said, "Alright," winked at us, and took us out.

The PM stormed out ahead of us, heading the wrong way. We looked at him all puzzled: why was he so angry?

"Hey Harry," called Jess to the PM, "this way," she pointed. He turned, smiled at her and followed like a puppy, falling in just behind us.

"How are Neave and Charles?" asked Rachael.

"Neave is doing fine, she a little fighter. She helps Emily look after the other kids; well ... she thinks she does," she smiled at the thought.

"Charles?" Rachael prompted.

"He's dead. The farm was attacked by the dead. He was On Stag and turned. Jason took him out." She went quiet.

It was the PM who asked the next question, which made us all stop and turn. "Fancy a drink tonight after we've chatted to Colonel Blimp?"

She smiled and said yes. We got to the block, and she showed us our rooms.

"I'll give you an hour, then fetch and take you back to the mess for food and drinks," said Jess as she left.

Two hours later, we were in a meeting room with Captain Smith. I'd asked if Tony, Jayne and Jackson could join us, but I found out Jackson had died in the attack along with his daughter. He was trying to save the children, which he did, to the end. At the head of the table was the PM. To his right was Jess, then me and Rachael. To his left was Captain Smith, Smith's second-in-command, Sergeant Goodman, and Tony and Jayne.

We all talked for quite some time, each group telling their story.

RAF Northolt, as we knew, was meant to be a refugee centre as it was ideally located, just off the M40. When the outbreak started, only the RAC were on site for some unknown reason. They awaited the arrival of survivors – but none came. The base had also been stocked with hardware. It could easily be doubled as a barracks for the forces, but again no one turned up.

Smith told us that there was enough food and water to last five years for the current number of people. It turned out to be twelve of the RAC and twenty civilians, the latter of which made their way there after the attack on the farm.

For over a year, Captain Smith and his twelve lived in peace, with only the odd dead coming to the gates and fences. They kept themselves to the buildings, so they wouldn't attract attention from the dead. They had tried the radios to see if anyone else was out there, but they didn't know how to work them – they were not trained for that.

The captain's people were new recruits; they were given the task of looking after the refugees. They were told a major force would be arriving but it didn't. It wasn't until Jess and her team came by that work started to happen. Tony sorted out the vehicles, and with what little I had taught them, they got the tanks and drones working.

There was a young lad in Jess' group who was a games buff. He taught himself how to work the drones. He started by doing little flights around the base, then further afield. It was with the drone that he saw my uber team coming up the M1 and to the hotel. After that, we moved on to the uber area: that's when a unit was sent out to stop us before we were attacked. They were a little too late; he lost us in the trees and didn't see the attack until it was underway. That's when he let two missiles off, then Jess' team moved in.

After the attack on the farm, Jess wanted to observe the uber. It puzzled her: why there were so many ... She, along with two others, went back to track them. What they saw scared the life out of them. The ubers would attack other dead groups – once they were bitten, they themselves turned into ubers. Jess got out of there as quickly as she could. She proclaimed that the area was a no-go zone. That is when they sent drones out to watch for survivors, but we were the first they saw. Jess said she knew it was me when we pulled into the hotel, and that's when she pulled a team together and went.

We had finally finished the briefing. We were going to turn in for the night then head back to London in the morning. Jess with Neave, along with Tony and Jayne and some of their people were coming, but others were staying. The PM was going to send a force in to help Captain Smith.

It was just as we were getting up that Tony spotted something on my neck.

I rubbed it, and that seemed to set it off itching. Rachael came up for a closer peek, and said it looked like a rash. Then she backed off with a look of horror on her face.

"Nick, you've been scratched, you're infected," she started to cry as did Jess. They both got closer and hugged me.

"But I didn't get touched, I'm sure," I said, starting to panic: I didn't want to be one of them, and neither did I want to die.

The PM turned to Smith, who had backed himself into a

corner, looking as if I had the plague. "Pull yourself together, man; he's fine, have you got a helicopter on the base?"

Smith couldn't take his eyes off me; the PM had to shout at him, which shook him out of his daze. He apologised and said, "Yes."

"Right," he turned to Tony, "can you prep it for takeoff ASAP?"

"Yes sir," and with that, he and Jayne ran out of the room.

"Nick, the hospital may have an antivirus made from your friend Paul's blood. It's not been tried yet, but we have to give it a go."

I was feeling a little overwhelmed with all that was going on. All I could do was nod. In myself, I felt great; I didn't feel ill or weak. It had been over six hours since the attack. Surely I should be feeling something, but I didn't.

"Make your way over to the heli, and I'll be with you soon. I'm going to radio the command centre and get everything sorted for when we fly in." He ran out of the room, then came straight back: "Smith, where's the radio room?" Smith went with him, seeming glad to get out of the same room as me.

Once outside, Jess ran off to tell Emily and Jason what was happening, and that she was off to London. They were to look after Neave until they travelled down to be with us. She was soon back, with tears still in her eyes. I told her to calm down and that I was alright.

"But you're not," she said, "you've been infected; I don't want to lose you again."

"Look, it's only a scratch, I should be dead by now, but I'm not. Maybe I'm like Paul and won't die."

She just went quiet. We got to the helicopter just as Tony was finishing refuelling it. Jayne came over, hugged me and said she was so sorry. I told her not to worry, and I'd be fine.

The PM came running up and said that the hospital was ready for me. Paul had sent a message: "About bloody time you came to visit!"

That made me smile.

We all climbed in the chopper. The PM took the pilot seat and started the engines. Within seconds we were in the air flying back to London.

Chapter Thirty-Seven

By the time we arrived at the hospital, the rash on my neck had spread. It was a dark blue and red, and you could see the veins enlarging. My vision was blurring; Rachael said that it looked like I had cataracts. I was taken to a room and hooked up to an intravenous drip that pumped a strong antibiotic into my system. I was told that this only slowed the infection and was not a cure. I sat in my bed with Rachael and Jess at my side. I tried to keep calm for them. Other than my eyes, I still felt healthy. The doctors agreed that this was a good sign. Two hours later, my sight seemed to return, and the doctors were happy with that.

The antivirus they were developing was on its way, I was told. The PM came to see me a couple of times, asking how I was. He would sit next to Jess, trying to reassure her. He even held her hand and she let him. At one point, I did give him a *that's-my-daughter* stare, but he smiled and kept a hold of it.

Surely this wasn't happening: a Prince of England, now the leader of a post-apocalyptic world, liked my daughter. This would have never happened before, but this is what the crazy, new world had done – brought strangers together in a fight for the common good. Okay, there were still the odd pocket of crazies, like Duncan, but they wouldn't last long.

Finally, the antivirus arrived, and they injected it into my intravenous drip. My blood seemed to boil as it entered; I was getting hot, sweat was pouring off my body. My arms started to shake, then my legs were twitching. My body followed suit – the pain was intense, I was sure my head was going to explode any minute.

I turned to Rachael who was on her feet. She was shouting something, I couldn't tell what. My vision went black, as something cool was put on my head. I started to panic; I didn't know it was a wet cloth. My throat was getting sore – I must have been screaming, but didn't know it. My sight came back as the cloth was removed. All I could see were blurred images of Jess and Rachael. I could feel the shaking getting worse, the pain in my head had reached its climax. That's when I fainted.

My dreams were of people being pulled apart. I saw Jess and Neave having their limbs eaten. I tried to fight my way to them; I had to save them from this horror. When I got to them, it was them that were eating other people. I had to kill them, but had nothing to do it with.

Looking for a weapon changed the scene in my mind. I was back at the castle – hoards of monsters had cornered me. The only place to go was the moat, but when I looked down into it, it was a pit full of dead bodies. Rotting and crawling with maggots, rats scurried in and out of the corpses. Snakes were slithering out of eye sockets.

As I turned away from the moat, there was Duncan, walking towards me, grinning a dead grin. I had to close my eyes; I couldn't take any more of this place. I heard my name called, it sounded close so I opened my eyes.

I don't know how, but I was on my back, and Paul was looking at me worriedly. He turned away and shouted, "He's awake!" and then looked back at me. "Bloody hell, mate, you had us worried. You're okay now, just relax," he said.

I was in the hospital bed, was I still dreaming or was I awake? I tried to ask, but my throat wouldn't work – it came out as a hiss. Movement made me turn, it was Jess and Rachael. Following them was the PM. Outside the door, I could make out Kelly, her eyes were red as if she had been crying.

Rachael came over and said that I had been out for three days, screaming and shouting. They had all taken turns watching me, waiting to see if I would come out of it or die. I couldn't believe what she was saying ... so I wasn't in a dream now. I started to remember what had happened. I signed, asking for a drink, and I gulped down the cold water. I still felt hot, but I was alive, other than Paul, the longest survivor.

Over the next few days I was checked and rechecked. My temperature wasn't going down, so I was given cold bed baths. People were in and out all the time. My voice started to return after resting it for a few days, and I asked if I could have some paper. I wanted to write down my experience of the holocaust.

Jess brought Neave in to see me one day, and that little girl made me smile. She was telling me about this man who took her and mummy out in a helliwopper, and how it made her tummy feel funny. I asked Jess who this man was, knowing full well. She just gave that *dad, you-bastard* look. I kissed them both goodbye. I tried to work out how long I had been infected; it was about seven days – wow. I was starting to feel tired and I slept a lot; still, people would be there when I woke up.

After one sleep, I awoke to find the PM there sitting, reading a book. When I moved, I noticed his hand go for his knife. Shit, I thought, I am dying; they are waiting for me to go.

The PM stood over me and smiled, "Sorry Nick, I didn't want you to see that, but you went quiet," he said.

"That's alright," I said, "I have done the same," I replied.

"I know that this isn't the time, but I need to ask you a question," he said, with all seriousness on his face.

"I've fallen for your daughter. She is the person I could live with; and who would treat me as an individual, not *what* I am."

I nodded, trying to give my father stare, but I didn't think it was working.

"I want to marry her, and I know she loves you a lot, and I know she would want me to ask you first. So, Mr Hutchinson, could I please have your daughter's hand in marriage?"

It brought a tear to my eye: this was the kind of man that I wanted as a son-in-law.

"Will you keep her and Neave safe? Would you treat Neave as if she was your own child?" I asked.

He said, "Yes, but you know Jess, she would kill me if I tried to stop her doing what she wanted ..."

I laughed at his truthful answer and gave my blessing.

Epilogue

It was Paul Lancaster's turn to watch over Nick as he fell asleep. It was two-hours later when he finally died. Paul called the others into the room so they could pay their last respects. Jess had brought Neave in, as the little girl said she wanted to see her Granddad one last time. She kissed his head. Harry had his arm around Jess' shoulder and led her, crying, from the room. Steve and Kelly took Rachael away after she had kissed him. They all had tears falling down their cheeks. Tony and Jayne had said their goodbyes and left with Rose.

Paul sat down and waited. He didn't have to wait long: Nick's eyes opened and he turned, hissing at Paul, who then plunged Nick's own knife into his temple.

Paul was in floods of tears; he kissed his friend's forehead and left.

The world never recovered from the infection, but people still survived and kept the human race going. Rachael carried on in Nick's name, helping where she could. Jess and Harry had two children: two boys, the eldest was called Nicolas and the next was called William. They grew up along with Neave, fighting the dead.

They would become the next generation, fighting for life in the world that was dead.

THE END

About the Author

Mark Harris was born 15th January 1967. He has lived in Leicester all his life. After leaving school he had a series of jobs from factory worker, gardener to bus driver and is even a qualified dog trainer competing in agility with his dogs. In his early twenties he was in the Territorial Army for four years and toured the world. Now he lives the quiet life with his wife Tina, daughter Tatania, granddaughter Zoe and Miley his Springer Spaniel.